Arabel Wilbur Alexander

The Life and Work of Lucinda B. Helm

Founder of the Women's Parsonage and Home Mission Society of the M.E. Church,

South

Arabel Wilbur Alexander

The Life and Work of Lucinda B. Helm
Founder of the Women's Parsonage and Home Mission Society of the M.E. Church, South

ISBN/EAN: 9783337000349

Printed in Europe, USA, Canada, Australia, Japan

Cover: Foto ©Raphael Reischuk / pixelio.de

More available books at **www.hansebooks.com**

Lucinda B. Helm

THE LIFE AND WORK

OF

Lucinda B. Helm,

FOUNDER OF THE WOMAN'S PARSONAGE AND HOME
MISSION SOCIETY OF THE M. E. CHURCH, SOUTH.

BY

ARABEL WILBUR ALEXANDER.

We live in a new and exceptional age. America is another name
for opportunity. Our whole history appears like a last effort of
Divine Providence in behalf of the human race.—Emerson.

NASHVILLE, TENN.:
PUBLISHING HOUSE OF THE METHODIST EPISCOPAL CHURCH, SOUTH.
BARBEE & SMITH, AGENTS.
1898.

TO
THE WOMEN OF THE HOME MISSION SOCIETY
OF THE M. E. CHURCH, SOUTH.

PREFACE.

Lucinda B. Helm's relation to a movement which had its birth in her fertile brain, and has grown up under her leadership to be one of the most potent and efficient departments of the great Methodist Episcopal Church, South, makes it eminently appropriate that the story of her life and work should be told.

During her life she was urged by many to publish a full account of her work; but, although possessing the ability to lead and organize, to mold thought and direct energies, she had the modesty that shrank from this task, as became a lady of her gentle breeding.

The intimacy between her and the writer was such that conversations concerning the history and development of her work were frequent, and in one of these she expressed a desire that if the facts were ever given in permanent form it should be done by the author, adding: "When I am gone, I think perhaps God would use the record as a blessing." Thus, while wishing that a worthier pen might render this loving service, we trace with sacred feelings the footsteps of this peerless woman.

It has been a source of encouragement that so many requests have been made since her death for a preparation of her biography. Her host of friends throughout the Church desire to know more of the inner springs of a life that was so fair and beautiful in itself, and that brought such help and inspiration to thousands. In response this little volume goes forth with the prayer that its imperfections may be overlooked, and that it may contribute to the promotion of that cause for which she gave her life.

We wish to acknowledge with gratitude the assistance rendered by Miss Mary Helm, the late Dr. David Morton, and other friends.   THE AUTHOR.

INTRODUCTION.

THE mission of Christ to the world was to save it from sin; the mission of his followers is to give the story of this evangel to every creature. Early in life, even in girlhood, Miss Helm had received a vision of her Lord and his mission. She taught and superintended a night-school for negroes. Thus began the work of laboring in the kingdom of God, a work which grew from dropping a few seeds near her Kentucky home to the sowing beside all waters. In later years she had the privilege, among many other undertakings, of making the first donation for the establishment of a mission in Korea.

Wholesomeness of religious life is rare; some persons are consumed by zeal; others are apathetic and self-controlled. Asceticism is not yet dead; while on the other hand there are men and women who feed on the emotional and sensuous side of religious life. No one was ever better poised than was this woman. With an uncompromising adherence to the right, she was no Pharisee; and, with a courage of conviction which made her a fearless advocate of truth, she was no Puritan. There was in her a joyousness of faith and a buoyancy of spirit which carried constant sunshine.

How magnificently she was endowed for leadership! Out from the discipline of a remarkable mother's realm, and from the counsels of a father invested with the care of a great commonwealth, came this woman with a body as frail as a flower, but with the courage of a Deborah. Hers was a spirit so resolute that no infirmity could conquer it. Hers was a strength of will so powerful that difficulties melted away as mist before the morning sun. Consecration, sympathy, intellectual grasp and soundness of judgment characterized her life-work.

"Glimpses into the inner regions of a great soul do one good," wrote Amiel in his journal. "Contact of this kind strengthens, restores, refreshes. At the sight of a man we too say to ourselves : ' Let us also be men.' " It is appropriate that the author of this life-sketch should lead us along the unbeaten paths where many, who did not know Miss Helm personally, may come into closer touch with her remarkable life. As the author had learned to know and love her so well as a friend, their companionship in effort and fellowship in Christ make her eminently qualified for this work.

WALTER R. LAMBUTH.

CONTENTS.

—

LUCINDA BARBOUR HELM.

DECEMBER 23, 1839 —NOVEMBER 15, 1897.

Behold, what manner of love the Father hath bestowed upon us, that we should be called children of God! (*1 John iii. 1.*)

CHAPTER I.

ANCESTRY.

"When a firm, decisive spirit is recognized, it is curious to see how the space clears around a man and leaves him room and freedom."—Foster.

THE ancestry of Lucinda B. Helm may be traced back to an early period in the history of our country. Some of her forefathers, it is believed, could boast of patrician blood, while others possessed a nobility higher than that of birth or station—the nobility of personal character. The family was one of the most influential of those that originally settled the Old Dominion colony. The first in the direct ancestral line of which we have any definite record was Thomas Helm, the grandfather of the late Gov. Helm and great-grandfather of Lucinda B. Helm. In 1780 he, with his family, left Prince William County, Va., where he had been born and reared, and started to seek his fortune in the yet unexplored wilderness of Kentucky. They reached the falls of the Ohio (where the city of Louisville is now situated) in March, at which place he remained for about a year; but as his family suffered from diseases contracted there, he mounted his horse one morning and set his face in-

land, with the determination not to return until he
had selected a permanent abiding-place. On the
third day of his search he reached the foot of the
hill in the vicinity of the present village of Elizabethtown. This hill commands the site of the
place where he afterward lived and died, and
also of the cemetery where he is now buried, surrounded by his descendants to the fifth generation.

A singular circumstance is related in connection
with the selection made by Thomas Helm of his
future place of residence. Before leaving Virginia, but while deliberating on the subject of a re-
moval, he had dreamed of just such a spot as that
upon which his eye rested when he ascended the
hill to which we have referred. The very spring
at which he drank—rushing out of its rocky bed,
strong and clear—was as the visionary fountain
that had appeared to him in his dream. The co-
incidence startled him, and, although anything but
a superstitious man, he accepted the omen as a
happy one, and concluded to search no farther.

This grandfather of Gov. Helm was just the
kind of man to make his way in a new country.
Daring, active, and possessing tastes suited to the
life of a pioneer, he was soon the occupant of a
strongly built fort, which he had erected for the
protection of his family against the then frequent
predatory excursions of roving bands of Indians.
This fort was situated in the small valley which in-
tersects the hills traversing the farm now known as

"Helm Place." Although Thomas Helm and his wife came of good families, they did not regret the hardships encountered in the "wilderness" of Kentucky. Gradually the Indians left the state, and Mr. Helm built a comfortable house beside the old fort, which served them for a residence the remainder of their days.

When a boy Gov. Helm was a great favorite with his grandparents. His grandfather was the oracle of the neighborhood on all matters connected with the Revolutionary era and the Indian troubles of Kentucky. It was at the knee of his venerable progenitor that he drank in the history of his country, and learned to appreciate the sacrifices made by the patriot band that achieved our liberties. His maternal grandparents were John and Mary Larue, who had emigrated from the valley of the Shenandoah, Va., in 1784.

Mrs. Larue was a beautiful and gifted woman. The county in which they lived, adjoining Hardin County, was named for their family — Larue County. Their daughter, Rebecca Larue, was a babe when her parents came to Kentucky, having been born in Frederick County, Va. She afterward became the wife of George Helm and mother of Gov. John L. Helm.

No man in that section of country was more respected than George Helm. He filled, at different times, various offices, civil and legislative, in the service of his fellow citizens.

John Larue Helm, the father of Lucinda B.
Helm, was born on the 4th of July, 1802, at the
old Helm homestead on the table-land of "Mul-
drough's Hills," one and one-fourth miles north
of the village of Elizabethtown. The country at
that time was sparsely peopled. The war-whoop of
the red man had then scarcely ceased its echoes
through the forests, and herds of wild animals
wandered over woodland and prairie, fearlessly and
almost undisturbed. The country embraced a territory which is now divided into three counties and
parts of others, and the inhabitants consisting then
of a few hundred are now numbered by thousands.

John L. Helm lived with his parents and grandparents up to the age of sixteen, and for about
eight years attended various schools in the neigh-
hood. With a mind naturally bright and strong,
and remarkable habits of industry, his advancement in knowledge was swift and easy. He was
at his books in the morning before others had
arisen, and long after they were sleeping at night
he was at them again, storing his mind with the
wisdom of the past. Before the age of sixteen he
had a knowledge rarely acquired by men at that
period of the history of his country and the character of its institutions. He had scarcely reached
the age of twenty when death deprived him of his
father, and he was not only thrown upon his own
resources for subsistence and further necessary education, but suddenly found himself the main sup-

port of his mother and the younger children. This
phase of the bereavement, however, proved to be
a blessing in the making of his magnificent man-
hood. The members of the family found their
hearts more closely drawn together in their afflic-
tion, and, mutually striving to lessen each others'
burdens, they lived on in hope of a better future.
This came at last, principally through the un-
flagging energy of the elder son. His nobility
of character was further exemplified by his
assumption, a few years later, of the entire in-
debtedness of his father's estate, which he paid
off out of the first-fruits of his legal profession.
After he had become prominent in political circles,
and a man of some means, he became very much
attached to a young lady, who was the daughter
of Hon. Ben Hardin, one of the most celebrated
lawyers and orators that Kentucky has ever produced. At one time Mr. Hardin was an opposing
attorney to a lawyer from Pennsylvania in an important case. The Pennsylvanian found himself
so badly discomfited in the contest that he soon
returned to his native state. His name was James
Buchanan, afterward President of the United
States. Mr. Hardin had a pleasant home that had
become the accustomed stopping-place of Methodist ministers. He used to say: "My wife is a
member, and I am an outside pillar of the Methodist Church."

This young lawyer, Mr. John Helm, made fre-

2

quent visits to the home of Hon. Ben Hardin, and laid siege to the heart of his eldest daughter, Lucinda. She was a beautiful young girl, with rare intellectual gifts. He had met her accidentally one day when he had called to see her father on business. She was only fourteen years of age then, and while he was in the parlor she went in to show her father a map she had drawn. All of her studies were under the immediate supervision of her father, to whom she was devoted. Mr. Helm said he loved her at first sight. There was something irresistible about her even at that early age. As she grew older she was still more attractive, and her career as a young lady was a brilliant one. She spent several winters with her father at the capital, and also in visiting Mrs. Maj. William Preston and other women of prominent social standing in Louisville. An extremely rich man sought to gain her affections, but she said he had very little sense, and she realized then how intolerable a married life would be for her unless the virtues of the man lay in his character rather than in his estates. Mr. John Helm persevered in his attentions to her for seven years; but at the end of that time he claimed her for his own, and they were married at Bardstown, Ky., in 1830. The happy and gifted young couple went to Elizabethtown, while Mr. Helm began to build their elegant residence in which they ever afterward lived. This residence, situated about one and one-fourth miles from Elizabethtown, and known as "Helm Place," is still the home of their children. The entrance to the grounds is about a fourth of a mile from the house, the approach to which is made beautiful by an overarching avenue of Scotch fir-trees, which continue to the summit of the hill, where it opens into a circle leading to the house. It is a typical "old Kentucky home," built of brick, with spacious rooms and broad verandas.

Mrs. Helm was delighted at the prospect of keeping house in their beautiful new home. The sterling worth of her character could hardly be overestimated. She was a devoted and helpful wife, and as her husband steadily rose to prominence she was his most fitting companion.

With a noble ancestry, equal to that of her husband's, she was by birth and every right which society recognizes entitled to all the social prestige that can be given one. Tall, stately, and handsome, she was indeed a queen among women, a noticeable figure in any assemblage of cultured and elegant people.

In the relation of mother she showed such wisdom and beauty of character that her large family of children were devoted to her, and have kept her before their memory all down the years as their ideal of womanhood. She was such a potent factor in molding the characters of her eleven children that we insert a few pen pictures of her methods and her home associations.

The subject of this biography has stated repeatedly that she owed all the worth of her character to the teachings of her wonderful mother. The noblest attributes of that mother's womanhood, the brilliant luster of her intellect, the charms and graces of social culture—all found their highest expression through her motherhood. Its responsibilities, cares, joys, and privileges superseded all else with her. Her sons held all womanhood in chivalrous reverence, because they accepted her as its type; while her daughters felt that with such a type before them they must needs aspire to the highest to reach her standard, and to fall below was to fail in life.

Miss Mary Helm, in writing of her mother, says:

"Instead of my mother pining for the opportunities of social life, from which she became in a measure debarred by her large family of children and by living in her country home, she made that home bright by her wonderful flow of joyous spirit, humor, and repartee. There was no such thing as a dull hour when mother was in the house; in her absence, the sun was in eclipse. In our childhood she was the merry companion of our games; as school children she gave a strict supervision to our studies. After lessons were over, in the evening came those delightful hours of reading and conversation that I shall never forget. Ah! Christopher North never presided over more delightful *noctes ambrosianæ*. Her knowledge was *lavished*

upon her children, who thrilled under her exquisite reading from the master minds of literature, or
glowed with the ardor that longed to emulate as
she recounted the deeds of the world's heroes. I
can never forget how my childish heart swelled
until it overflowed in tears as she told us of Martin
Luther before the Diet of Worms. Moral courage she held the highest, yet to fail in physical
courage was a disgrace.

"My mother was given to hospitality, entertaining with a grace and dignity that made her an
elegant as well as charming hostess. Parties, teas,
and dinings of the formal kind were frequent; but
what she enjoyed most was the informal coming
together for the day of her chosen friends. There
were many occasions when, for weeks at a time,
the only limit to the guests was when the last bed
was full. Her children were also at full liberty to
fill the house with their friends; and, whether they
were old or young, she was the center of attraction
for them as well as for her own family, and enjoyed all the fun as much as any one else in the
house.

"My mother was a born commander, without
the slighest element of a tyrant. Not only her
own children, but everybody's children obeyed her.
They could not help it, and they did not want to
help it. Consistent, prompt, and systematic, she
had well-defined laws for governing her family and
house. My father left all domestic matters entire-

ly to her.   His admiration for her was unbounded.
What she did could not have been better done;
what she said was beyond question the right thing.
With the children he was always her stanch sup-
porter, never entertaining for an instant any appeal from her decision. Besides raising eleven
children to maturity, and giving them attention in
every line, she was a most thorough housekeeper,
and trained her servants to perfection, not only
for present service, but the young for the future.
Cooks, laundresses, waiters, maids, and seam-
tresses all received their training from her personally.   It was a fine model of an industrial
school, and all were devoted to her.

   " Every spring and fall she cut out with her
own hands all the garments worn by the negro
women and children, and the shirts for the men
(my father owned sixty negroes); she attended to
the picking of the wool, the spinning, and the
knitting into socks or weaving into cloth. By her
servants (the word ' slave ' was never heard) she
was regarded as something beyond human. Besides training them in material things, she instilled
moral and religious truth in every way possible.
She encouraged their confidence, but never
brooked familiarity. Quick to defend one who
was mistreated or oppressed, she was the *Cour
of Appeals* for final settlement of every case
where overseer, parents, children, or the strong
abused their power. When sickness came she

nursed them all with tender carefulness. At one time there were five of her own children and ten of the negroes very ill with scarlet fever, and she gave every dose of medicine day and night, going with a lantern from cabin to cabin all through the night; and so successful was her care that all recovered.

"For years Sister Lucinda was almost an invalid, needing her care day and night; and later, when I became a helpless sufferer for many years, she went through it all again. For eighteen months she was never out of the sound of my voice, and for five years never left me for longer than an hour. During all that time she kept up my despairing heart with her indomitable courage and unfailing hope, turning my morbid thoughts to brighter things outside of self, leading them into fields of literature and art, history and fancy. She was the most wonderful combination of an encyclopedia and a magician! But when the darkest hours would come, and my rebellious soul refused its God, with a firm hand she held my spirit in check while her own faith took hold on God in prayer. Oh, those prayers! I have never heard anything like them. They had to be answered, and *they were*."

Thus this grand, broad-natured woman gave herself to her children in such a way that in after-years they naturally became distinguished for their mental and moral worth.

The eldest son, Ben Hardin Helm, educated at West Point, afterward a lawyer of high standing, was finally a brigadier-general in the Confederate service, and fell at the battle of Chickamauga. In 1861 he became a brother-in-law to President Lincoln, having married Mrs. Lincoln's sister. The President, who was his personal friend and admirer, offered him the position of quartermaster-general of the United States army at the beginning of the civil war; but Mr. Helm declined, tendered his services to the Confederacy, and was killed when in command of what was known as the "Orphan Brigade."

Lizzie Barbour Helm, their eldest daughter, married Hon. H. W. Bruce, who was a member from Kentucky of the first permanent Congress of the Confederate States, and is at present chief attorney of the Louisville and Nashville Railroad.

George Helm, now dead, was a lawyer, and a man of very noble character.

Their fifth daughter, Emily Palmer Helm, married Martin Hardin Marriott, who died young, [and she has for two years managed the Industrial Department of the Scarritt Bible and Training School, in Kansas City, Mo.]; while Misses Mary and Lucinda Helm have been known and loved in Methodist Church circles all over our Southland for many years. Thus is strikingly shown that for generations back the Helm family has been distinguished for strength of mind and nobility of charac-

ter.   These qualities were illustrated in a marked
degree by the beloved founder of the Woman's
Home Mission Society of the M. E. Church, South.
With the mind of a lawyer and the heart of a saint,
she gave her remarkable intelligence, energy, and
faith to the establishment of a work that has iden-
tified her inseparably with the history of American
Methodism.

CHAPTER II.

GIRLHOOD.

"No one is born into this world whose work is not born with him."
—Lowell.

IT was said by Lucinda Helm's mother that she believed little Lucinda was converted before she could talk, so marked was her individuality even in infancy, and so devout her instincts before they could hardly be called "beliefs." Prayer was to her little mind a most sacred thing, and she became conscious of a higher Power in her life almost as soon as she was conscious of her mother. When as a very small child she was wilful or obdurate, she could not be corrected as the other children, but the mention of God in prayer made her perfectly submissive and obedient. Before she was old enough to go to school she taught herself to read, and the Bible was her text-book.

It was a matter of remark by the other members of the family that little Lucinda, a mere prattling infant, should open the old family Bible, and at her mother's knee learn the letters and spell out the words.

She writes in later years of the joy she experienced in the gift of her *first Bible.* She says: " When I was very small my father brought home one day some Bibles. He gave each of my two older sisters one, and I thought that was all; they were always coupled together. But there was one more. When I took in the idea it was for *me* I sprang up with a bound of joy. My mother had told us stories out of her big Bible, and now I had a little one all my own! I shall never forget my delight as I hugged it to my heart, or my father's merry laugh at my impulsiveness. How I loved that Bible, loved to find the stories, loved to know my father brought it to *me!* With what zest I repeated the lines:

> Holy Bible, book divine,
> Precious treasure, thou art mine!

Many times in after-years in the agony of sorrow I have soothed myself to sleep by holding it to my heart as I did that first day it came to me when a little child."

The honesty, simplicity, and frankness that characterized her during her entire life was strikingly prominent in her childhood. Absolutely faithful to her convictions of right and wrong, even in childhood, she resolutely refused to compromise any matter of principle, and would endure with unflinching steadfastness popular disfavor, if need be, to maintain the right. She has told us that when childish difficulties arose in play she invariably chose the side of the weak ones or those in disfavor, and used every means her little brain could devise to properly balance things. A ver-

itable peacemaker and missionary she was from
the beginning. Her love for books and study was
all-absorbing. *Everything* interested her. The
world was a sort of fairy-land, out of which she
would often weave wonderful stories, to the great
delight and entertainment of her child friends.
She never had robust health after she was four
years old, and when she was eight the family physician told her mother that she might die any moment from heart-disease or she might possibly live
for fifty years.

Although often prostrated by illness and always
very delicate, she advanced rapidly at school.
When but a little child she stood at the head of a
class of nearly grown boys and girls, her blue
eyes sparkling with intellectual ambition, while
her poor, weak heart beat so hard and fast that
her little white apron would quiver from its puls-
ing. Many times she had to run aside from her
frisking, romping playmates, and rest under the old
apple-trees in their shady back yard. One would
hardly have thought, seeing her then so sweet and
fragile like the blossoms that fell upon her, that
she would after all have a career of wider usefulness than any of her companions. The favorite
playground for the children was a large garden
back of the house; and as their mother was a natural florist and horticulturalist, their yard was brilliant with flowers and shrubs from early spring
until snow.

The old-fashioned garden was divided into squares, each square bordered with flowers of every variety, and there were summer-houses densely covered with honeysuckles and grape arbors.

Little Lucinda loved the old-fashioned flowers: the daffodils and morning-glories. The wide, well-kept walks made splendid race-tracks for the children and their friends in the neighborhood. In the lower part of the yard was a large spring, and the brook that flowed from it was to them enchanting in its sparkling beauty. They made sailing-vessels in which they fancied themselves " storm-tossed and wrecked on cannibal islands."

Lucinda could excel all the others in making cataracts and sailing her little bark boats as she accompanied them with wonderful made-up fairy tales of adventure about them and their crew. She was so imaginative, and read so many stories from "Arabian Nights" and other child-lore, that she was unanimously chosen as the best at making up stories, half the charm of them being in the fact that she and the others too were so carried away in fancy that for the time being it was reality to them.

All the children had their little negro maids, who played with them, and Lucinda was much attached to hers, and continued so until the maid's death, which occurred soon after she became free.

An important personage, who figured largely in

the home of her childhood, was old Aunt Gilly. She was nurse to all the eleven children; but little Lucinda was preeminently her " chile," partly because her ill health so frequently made her require a nurse's care.

The children often had " night-schools " in a small way for the negroes, and here Lucinda was in her element, especially on Sunday afternoon, at which time she was superintendent and principal teacher. At their prayer-meetings they would get her to come and read the Bible for them, then they prayed one after another, and when they prayed lovingly for " little Miss Cindy," who had read God's Word to them, it made her very happy. She says in speaking afterward of those days: " They continually looked to me for this service. If one of the older ones sat spelling out the words in her Testament on a quiet Sabbath afternoon, it came very natural for me to sit down by her, take the book, and read the precious words to her. I learned to find the most comforting passages that told of God's wonderful love and his bright promises of the ' happy land of Canaan.' "

Of those early years of ministry to the negro servants and others she again says: " More times than I can count did God speak through my child lips to the blind, the sick, the sinful, the sorrowing, the old, the dying—speak to their hearts through me with a meaning I could not then comprehend,

though the words passed my lips. It was God
speaking to them, not I. He was using my voice
to say his own words.''

When she was about eleven years old her father
became Governor of the state, succeeding J. J.
Crittenden, who resigned to accept a place in
President Taylor's cabinet. He removed his
family at this time from their country home near
Elizabethtown to the seat of government at Frank-
fort. Here she was brought into contact with un-
accustomed gaiety, calculated to fascinate a young
and ardent nature, but she was glad when the
family returned at the end of a year to their beautiful old home. Her father, after serving the first
term as Governor, applied himself to his profession for the three years following, and then
became President of the great Louisville and Nashville Railroad, of which he was practically the
originator. The first train that crossed the Roll-
ing Fork into his native county bore the President of the road. He was a proud man that
day, and justly so. He had lived to serve the material interests of his people, to see his own beloved county wedded to the beautiful Ohio, fifty
miles away, and his heart dilated with a sense of
pleasure as his lifelong friends and neighbors,
from the positions they had taken up beside the
track all along the course, waved to him their
congratulations as he was swiftly borne on his
way to Elizabethtown. How proud little Lucinda

was of her "great" father! She wrote a beautiful little article when she became older, and called it "My Father," showing how his love was to her typical of the fatherhood of God.

Although she frequently took the leadership in play with other children, she was by nature sensitive and shrinking. Her bravery was always the bravery of *nerve*. The make-up of her character was particularly attractive and sweet to her brother George, who was dearer to her than her own life. She began to study drawing and painting, and developed much talent in that direction. He was very proud of her work. For hours they would wander together over the wooded hills or through the overarching avenue of Scotch fir-trees with her sketchbook in hand, selecting scenes for her sketches suitable to their tastes. His character was pure and exalted, and accompanied always by a chivalry equal to a knight of old. Lucinda thought him perfect, and lavished the strength of her affection upon him. The first great sorrow that ever touched her life was the death of this brother, which occurred when she was about sixteen. For a time she felt completely lost. No one could take the place of her beloved brother George. Having loved with such devotion a man of his character, she involuntarily measured all other young men she met after that by his standard.

As she blossomed into young womanhood her sweet face, winsome manners, and intelligent con-

LUCINDA HELM AT THIRTEEN.

versation made her much sought for and admired. She enjoyed at that period, as well as in later life, intellectual and cultured society. She put no narrow restrictions about a religious life, but at the same time stood firm for the maintenance of certain principles in those who professed to be Christians. She was fond of horseback riding and of shooting-parties, but she refused to dance or engage in any games that seemed to her inconsistent with a right Christian life. During this period, although she might have chosen many times a future in which ease and pleasure would have been hers, her predominant ambition was, as in her childhood, to be useful to her friends and associates.

When Lucinda was eighteen years old she quietly made up her mind to join the Church. She did not at this time experience any definite change of heart. This troubled her considerably, but she said: " I certainly love God above and beyond all things else in life, and I can not remember the time when I did not." When she was told that many of the best and holiest men and women in the Church could not give any clearer evidence of their conversion than that, she ceased to fear, and trusted. Her definite choice for God at this period, when a life of gaiety and ease was offered to her on all sides, made a marked impression on her associates. She said that her refusal to dance often gave her the coveted opportunity to speak of Christ to young men over whom

she exerted much influence. Yet there was never
a trace of " sanctimoniousness " or " cant " in her
word or manner. Her religion was from the beginning to the end of her life a genuine, natural
acceptation of God as her Father, and this conviction was as deep and all-absorbing in the molding of her character as if she had fought for it
amid throes of doubt and unbelief and rebellion.
Her faith was so ingrained in her nature even before she experienced the ecstatic joy that came
later, that for one to refute the fatherhood of God
was in her sight to undermine all truth that gave
hope to the world.

One social evening there were several young
men present, one of whom was especially gifted
and intellectual. He was very much attached to
Miss Lucinda, and she admired him except for
his absence of all spirituality. In the course of
the conversation he began to advance skeptical
views—views which she heard him express for the
first time. At first her face quivered with pained
surprise, but as he went on she began to combat
his arguments with historical and scriptural proofs.
Growing more and more earnest, she became
unconscious of herself, and with uplifted head,
her cheeks glowing, and her eyes brilliant as stars,
she grew eloquent in proving to them that Christ
was the Son of God. This was but one example
of her loyalty to God anywhere and under any
circumstances.

There was a definite set time soon after this incident in which it fully dawned on her that her ideals of earthly happiness as she had dreamed of them and wondered about them, and grew lovely at the very thought of their rose-tinted beauty, could never be realized. These sacred pages of her life recounting the struggles of a high, lofty soul with *self* we shall not scan, but the outcome proved her to be conqueror. For several years there was a sweet, pensive longing for something that would give expression and currency to the throbbings of her eager spirit. Sweet, young, and gifted, yet she was not satisfied with the pleasures of the world. Her great heart had weighed them and found them wanting. She shut herself up alone one day. It was a golden eventide, and a tremulous stillness pervaded the place. She spent hours in meditation and prayer. The surrender of herself—soul, mind, and body—to her Heavenly Father was complete. All her desires, plans, hopes, ambitions, were given entirely to him. A voice seemed to speak to her: "Thy Father loves thee with a jealous love. He wants thee now and forever *all to himself.*" The words were like a triumphant burst of music to her spirit. She was filled with ecstasy. She arose and said: "It shall be! I will be his as never before. His work shall be mine, his creatures shall be mine to love, to serve, to save." Her spirit was illumined like that of the Maid of Orleans in the prophetic

vision of what she might do for her divine
Lord.

Nothing looked impossible. The possibility of
most untoward circumstances only spoke a larger
hope to her elated spirit. She did not really see
the streak of sunlight on the floor. She was in-
wardly seeing the light of years to come and feeling the way they might be filled with joyful de-
votedness. Under the rush of solemn emotion in
which thoughts became vague, she could but cast
herself with a childlike sense of reclining into
the lap of divine consciousness which sustained
her own.

In the days that followed a great peace was in
her heart, and a light in her face that kept it radiant. She was possessed by the fact that a fuller
life was opening for her. She was going to have
room somewhere for the energies which stirred
uneasily within her, and which nothing she had ever
known had yet satisfied. The realization that God
loved her with a close, jealous love fired her spirit
to live on the heights and to stay there, and so she
did. Soon after that she had a beautiful dream,
which she relates as follows: " I stood alone in a
church. The closed doors shut out every sound
of life. The bare, cold walls lifted themselves
high above me. The dim evening light came
through the tall, somber windows and fell upon the
empty pews ranged in their long lines as still as
though no motion or sound of life had ever passed

through them. All was still, and I was there alone
—a part, as it were, of the great stillness. The
sudden consciousness that I was in the temple of
the living God filled my soul with awe. I felt that
I stood in the outer courts of God's great presence-
chamber; that I was near the unseen, the mighty,
the holy God. I felt the majesty of his power.
My heart beat low. I scarcely breathed as I
looked toward the altar where his word lay closed,
clasped. But from its passive presence by the
wordless influence of the Holy Spirit there glided
into my soul a great consciousness of God's love,
of the crucified One who through blood and tears
told of this love. God had come into his temple
softly, and as a loving Saviour had drawn near to
me. Peace soothed my awe-bound heart, and my
spirit, freed from fear, was transfused with the
quiet, holy joy of love. I was in the presence of
One who loved me. The mighty God before whose
awful throne I bowed was *my Father!* He had
opened to me the doorway of his glorious abode.
I stood in the gateway of heaven, and the Son of
God was at my side! Holy peace, joy—aye, rapt-
urous gladness filled my spirit as, motionless, I
lifted my eyes to him that sitteth upon the throne
and my heart in boundless love echoed the praises
of those who stand ever before him crying, ' Holy,
holy, holy, Lord God Almighty, which was, and
which is, and which is to come.' ''

In the months that followed, a sweet, frail girl

possessed by a noble ambition might have been
seen every Sunday afternoon walking alone a
mile in the country to an old farmhouse to hold
an afternoon service. Men, women, and children
from the country round about gathered to hear
her. As she stood before them so quietly with
her open Bible in her hand looking out over the
little crowd of hungry-hearted people and speaking to them words of hope and salvation, it was to
them like a visitation from heaven. They flocked
about her and told her their troubles and their
secret fears. She comforted them and pointed
them to the perfect Love that casteth out fear.
No measurements of earth could calculate the
results of those years of simple " wayside preaching." Her mother desired her to visit one winter
in Louisville, but upon arriving there, instead of
going into a round of social gaieties, she went to
one of the principal city missionaries, Mrs. Sad,
offered her services, and during that entire winter
proved one of her most faithful assistants. She
learned in that early training much practical
knowledge of city evangelization. But great
trials and sorrows came to her when the civil war
broke out. Their beautiful home of wealth and
culture was invaded and their property taken. Her
oldest brother went into the service of the Confederacy and was killed, and for a time her loved
father was made prisoner, having been rudely
taken from his home. Their slaves, some of

whom were dear to her heart, were scattered, and
sorrow and loss were felt everywhere. The
hearts of her father and mother were nearly
broken at the death of their noble son, and Lucinda
felt that their multiplied griefs must be a spur to
her faith and Christian activity.

She went to work. She became correspondent
for a large paper published in England called the
Western News, and sent frequent letters to it giving war items, etc. She suffered anxiety, priva-
tion, and sorrow; but with great zeal she worked,
making lint and bandages for the wounded and
clothes for the prisoners. The long-continued
strain so affected her nervous system that she
came near losing the sight of her eyes, and for
more than a year faced the possibility of blindness. What a year of sorrow was that! Besides the physical suffering, which was sometimes excruciating, and besides the inexpress-
ible horrors and uncertainties of living in the
midst of *war*, she faced the very possible future
of a life of blindness; and her vivid imagination
pictured for her the long months and years of
darkness dragging out their heavy length and
bringing to her only the commiseration of her
friends—commiseration—that was always so dis-
tasteful to her. Yet her faith wavered not. It
was an extreme test, but she arose equal to it,
and said to her Lord and Master: "This matter
is settled between thee and me. Shall I receive

good from the hand of my Lord, and not evil? If
this is *thy* will concerning me, it is well." But it
proved to be not his will, and, after going through
heroic treatment, she recovered. Three years
after the close of the war, and immediately prior
to her father's death, he was again made Governor of the state, the inauguration taking place
on his death-bed. This was an impressive and
long-to-be-remembered scene. Preparations had
been made in the town for a grand display.
Special trains brought in large numbers of friends
and political admirers from Louisville, Frank-
fort, and other cities and towns of the state, all
anxious to witness the inaugural ceremonies. At
eleven o'clock a procession was formed in the
town, and, preceded by a band of musicians,
took up its march toward "Helm Place." Before they had gone half the distance they were
met by one of the physicians, who begged them
to stop. He said the music and shouting would
excite his patient to such a degree as to render
him physically unable to undergo the fatigue of
the ceremony in which he had necessarily to
take a part. Only those officers of state whose
presence was necessary were permitted to enter
the sick-room. The inauguration of the dying
patriot was a pathetic sight. Propped up in his
bed, his features worn and haggard from dis-
ease and his hands lying in weakness beside him,
it was a scene that filled the hearts of his devoted

wife and children with anguish. But the old strong spirit shone out of his eyes, and he spoke to his friends as they approached his bedside, expressing his pleasure at their presence. On one side of the bed stood the dignitaries who were to administer the oath of office to him, and on the other side stood the loving wife and the attending physicians, while grouped around were the members of his family, his two sons-in-law, and a few intimate friends. While the oath of office was being administered every one listened in breathless silence, and were duly impressed with the solemnity of the occasion.

The following Friday morning he was dying. His family, a few intimate friends, and some of the old family servants were gathered together in the room. His brother read the Bible and prayed while they knelt about his bed, after which he asked the dying man if he was trusting in God. He answered " Yes " so clear and loud that it was heard distinctly throughout the room. To those dearest to him he had before professed his faith in Christ, but had not done so publicly up to this time. His daughters went forward and each imprinted a kiss upon his pallid lips; and the wife— the faithful, devoted wife—bent over him and said in broken accents: " Kiss me once more, my husband." He pressed his lips to hers and kissed her for the last time. One more day he lingered, being hardly alive, and on Sabbath morning, as they watched by his side, his spirit departed to be with its God. Miss Lucinda was about twenty-eight years old at the time of her father's death. It marked an epoch in her life. Many changes came in the home, and she gave herself definitely to religious work in a fuller measure even than before. Her love for God and his cause broadened and deepened until like a holy fire it consumed every other wish and thought.

CHAPTER III.

"In the measure in which thou seekest to do thy duty shalt thou know what is in thee. But what is thy duty? The demand of the hour."—Goethe.

A VERY prominent element in Miss Lucinda Helm's character, and one that made her especially successful in missionary work, was her practical good sense.

Being as a girl imaginative and full of dreams and fancies, one would hardly expect to find that clear-sightedness and excellent " common sense " that always characterized her as a Christian worker. She did not brood over the past nor build "air-castles" for the future, but got her lesson from each passing hour. Her devotion to Christ had crystallized into a set purpose to forward his kingdom in the world, and with St. Paul she could truthfully say: *"This one thing I do!"*

In all her writings for papers, both secular and religious, her style is noticeably clear and strong, and in her personal work her fine discrimination and good judgment, combined with a heart so full of Christian love that it could take in and " mother" all who came to her, made her a spiritual force.

"There is no time," she used to say, "for specu-
lations on questions that make no essential difference concerning the present or the hereafter.
Our religion is a matter of life and death, and the
world is perishing for the want of Christian help.
Let us reach out our hands in blessing; let us lose
no time in our service for Christ." This spirit of
earnestness and concentration made every work,
no matter how dull and lifeless it had been or
looked to be, blossom under her touch.

She was remarkably successful as a Sunday-
school teacher, and had much faith in the power of
childhood. She formed various societies and liter-
ary "clubs" where she found it at all practicable,
for she believed organized effort to be an important factor in social and religious economics.
One "society" known in Elizabethtown only by
the name of "Miss Lucinda's Society" was composed of small boys, the simple pledge of membership being that they would not use profane or
indecent language and not play marbles for
"keeps." Its influence for purity of thought and
word among those young boys could not be calculated. Rev. David M. Sweets, now pastor of
Portland Avenue Presbyterian Church, in Louisville, says concerning this little society: "I pre-
sume I was not more than ten years old when I
was made secretary of the society. We used to
meet in the old schoolhouse, and a great many
boys attended. We all loved Miss Lucinda very

much, and her influence among the boys was
great. The object of the society was to train the
boys into leading a practical Christian life, and
the Boys' Branch of the Y. M. C. A. of Elizabethtown grew out of it. The memory of her unselfish life and loving interest in us will ever be an influence for good in my life, and I am sure many
more of her ' boys ' would say the same.''

The method of Christian work that Miss Helm
especially emphasized by tongue and pen was
personal effort in the saving of souls. Her unusual tact and judgment made her very efficient in
direct appeals to the unsaved. She says in an article entitled "Apples of Gold in Pictures of Silver," published in the *St. Louis Christian Advocate* in 1875:

" I was at one time frequently thrown in com-
pany with a talented but very old man with
whom I had many a merry chat before I knew
he was not a Christian. When I learned this
from some one else—for I am ashamed to say
I did not discover it for myself, having never
mentioned the subject to him—I said something to
him about his soul's salvation. He looked at me
earnestly with some surprise. 'You never spoke
to me that way before.' 'No,' I said, 'but I
should have done so.' He drooped his head and,
shaking it slowly, said sadly, ' I wish you had, my
dear young lady; I wish you had.' My heart
stood still as a sense of my neglect rushed over

me. He was very old—full fourscore, I think—yet
without the pale of salvation. His time was very
short indeed, and I, as if I had not known the
truth, had sought only to amuse him, my vanity
perhaps pleased that he was so well entertained by
what I said, and now as opportunity for doing
aught to save him was well-nigh gone, his sad,
gentle reproach was more than I could bear.

" Was it too late? Possibly not. Every energy
of my soul was aroused to the highest pitch. I
would be the means of saving him yet if God
would forgive and help me. Thanks be to God,
by his grace the work was done, and I had been
taught a lesson I shall never forget.

" We know not when our words may influence
our fellow beings for good or evil, but the word
must be spoken not only in due season, but ' fitly
spoken,' that it may be precious like ' apples of
gold in pictures of silver.' As I write these words
another friend comes before my mind's eye
whose experience may illustrate this truth further.
I knew and loved her in days gone by. She had
a sweet, sad face, and her voice was low with a
mournful cadence that, while it fell softly upon
my ear, pained my heart. Upon her face there
rested a shadow that troubled me. Wrapped in
her own sad thoughts, she stood aloof from others,
and I could not but watch her, irresistibly drawn to
love her while we were yet little more than strangers. Never shall I forget the shock I felt when

one who knew her came and whispered: 'She is an infidel.'

"An infidel? So sad, and no God to turn to, bearing her heavy burdens alone, without a Saviour to comfort! My first impulse was to go to her and throw my arms around her and tell her of Jesus' love, but I could not so recklessly break through the gentle reserve with which she surrounded herself. I endeavored quietly to draw her into conversation upon topics that might open a way for me to approach her, but she would say but little. I did not seek a discussion or argument upon abstract views of truth, for sorrow was so deeply written upon her face that I was convinced *reason* had little to do with the matter. The trouble lay altogether with the poor aching heart. Day after day I strove indirectly to reveal to her the blessedness of God's love, and at night when I lay down, like a burden upon my soul rested the fear that before morning she might stand in the presence of Him she had denied on earth, for I had been told that every night she lulled herself to sleep with small doses of laudanum. In the room adjoining mine an immortal soul might be leaving earth unprepared to meet its Creator. In the silence of the night I listened if I might catch any unusual sound, and when morning came great would be my relief to find there was yet time.

" But what could I say that I had not said? For, although I longed to know her sorrow, that I might

4

point her to Christ, I could not question nor ob-
trusively draw aside the veil behind which this
delicate nature strove to hide its sacred grief, and
yet without some further knowledge of the case
my words were like seeds thrown to the winds.
So I could only pray for her, and at last, in answer
to my fervent prayer, *God opened a way* for me.

  "One came running to me saying: 'Miss ——
is suffering from a sudden nervous attack, and I
do not know what to do for her.' By the time I
reached her the room was full of people. Some
were calling for remedies and some for the doctor.
She was hiding her face and trembling from head
to foot. Feeling satisfied that some new event had
been recorded in the sad history I had been striving to read, I went quickly to her, and laying my
hand lightly on hers, whispered: 'This is mental,
not physical, suffering.' I felt the quivering
nerves relax and grow quiet, and knew I had not
erred. 'You do not want a physician; you want
rest,' to which she assented.

  "Telling her friends she wished to be alone, I
silently strove to soothe her. The way was now
open. I had broken down the barrier between
us by words I had never thought of uttering.
From that hour she seemed to cling to me and
find relief in unburdening her sorrow-laden heart.
I found she acknowledged the existence of God,
but stood in open rebellion against him, because
his hand had touched the idol of her heart. She

thought that God took pleasure in torturing her poor, stricken soul!

"Some time after that, as I prayed and strove for her, she came one day to my room and with a fond word put a tube rose in my hair and timidly kissed me. Then I was glad, for I knew I had won. A heart that could feel a sweet gratitude for a few words of sympathy could not long resist the great love of the Saviour who died for her, and it was true. She yielded completely and gave her heart and life entirely to Christ. After this I said to myself: 'Now do I *know* when we are truly in earnest God will help us and teach us when and how to speak for him.'"

Miss Helm was a quick reader of human nature. This was one of the secrets of her power as an organizer. She could select and enlist by some intuitive process the most suitable coworkers in every department of work she undertook, and her native tact and gentleness of manner made it easy for any one to receive training from her.

When the Woman's Foreign Missionary Society was organized, in 1876, she was one of the most earnest and successful advocates of the cause. She believed in woman, and she believed there was no limit to what Christ would do for the world if we as his witnesses did our part. She would quote with deep earnestness and pathos those words of Bishop Galloway: "Upon this earth he has no hands but ours, no feet but ours, no lips

but ours, to herald his truth. How can we afford
to waste such opportunities?" She wrote for the
Woman's Missionary Advocate and for the Church
papers in the interest of foreign missions. She
took every means to become well-informed, and
her knowledge of the subject, accompanied by her
fervor of spirit, made her work excellent. She
took a great interest in the *Woman's Missionary
Advocate*, and while her sister, Miss Mary, was
Corresponding Secretary of the Louisville Conference, Miss Lucinda was the first in that Conference
to send to the Secretary a paid-up list of subscri-
bers. The Louisville Conference money was the
first received by Mrs. Manier (who was then the
agent), and she has said to her coworkers that but
for it she could not have met the expense of the
first issues of the *Advocate*. In all Miss Lucinda's
local work, both of a religious and social nature, her
loved sister, Miss Mary, was her companion and
coworker. After she became Secretary of the
Woman's Department of Church Extension, and
Miss Mary was Assistant Secretary of the Woman's
Foreign Missionary Society, they had adjoining
rooms, where they did their work, and gained
much help from mutual consultation, besides the
active help of attending each to the other's mail,
etc., in the absence of one or the other. Thus it
was that the two societies worked at that time hand
in hand and heart to heart.

Miss Lucinda edited the leaflets for the For-

eign Missionary Society, and in such an able manner as to contribute largely to the interest of the
work as it spread rapidly throughout the Church.
Many of her articles and leaflets, although nearly
twenty years old, would furnish excellent material
for missionary workers to-day. One article, entitled " Seed-Time," was published in the Nashville
Christian Advocate in 1880. In it she says:

" We often hear quoted, in connection with missionary work, ' The harvest truly is plenteous, but
the laborers are few.' While in one sense this is
true, it leaves an impression that is in a measure
the cause of discouragement in foreign missionary work.

" The impression made is that the harvest is ripe
and ready for the sickle, and we have but to send
reapers to gather in abundant sheaves of precious
souls, when the truth is it is still seed-time, and laborers are needed to go with brave, pioneer hearts
to fell the great trees, to break up and prepare the
ground for the seed they must sow, and leave to
others in the perhaps far future the joy of reaping
the harvest. And they should be content with
this, for if all would be reapers, there would be
no harvest to reap. And we who send out the laborers into the fields should be patient too, and
not discouraged because we see not great results
at once. What have we to do with the *results?*
The command to *us* is: ' In the morning sow thy
seed, and in the evening withhold not thine hand:

for thou knowest not whether shall prosper, either this or that, or whether they both shall be alike good.' There is another source of discouragement that has a most paralyzing effect: individuals are apt to feel that what they can do is so insignificant, and amounts to so little, that it might as well be left undone. This is a great mistake.

"Let one of the ladies in the smallest auxiliary of our Woman's Foreign Missionary Society—one quiet soul who throws her pennies with her heart into the work—compare her work and influence to a grain of wheat, a very little thing indeed. What could one poor, insignificant grain of wheat do in a great field? It is a plump, full grain, for a little deed done from sincere love to the Saviour is a perfect work. It is sown in rich earth ready for it. The Master watches it. By and by it grows and ripens, bearing many full grains, which in their turn fall, spring up again, and scatter a larger crop, and in time the single grain, the influence of a single humble life, has brought forth fruit a thousandfold. A touching incident before me further illustrates this. It was a time of fearful persecution. A heathen queen, drunk with the blood of God's saints and thirsting for more, was on the throne. Decree after decree had gone forth, and thousands were the victims that had fallen before her cruel rage. Almost every mouth was stopped through fear, and scarcely did any dare to speak the hated name of Jesus.

"In the queen's palace, and allied to the royal family, was a little girl. She knew no religion but the worship of idols. One nobleman believed in Jesus, and a holy boldness was his. He ventured to speak to the little child about her soul and of the true God, and of his Son, who was sent into the world to save sinners. His earnest words made an impression, but the worthy man never saw any fruit. He sowed in bloody times. The harvest did not come in his day. But a few years rolled away, and behold! the court of the palace is open and a multitude throng to see a sight never before witnessed in that land. A queen who bore the same name as the bloodthirsty queen that had put to death thousands of her subjects was about to profess her faith in the Christian's Saviour.

"She was questioned as to her acquaintance with this religion of the heart, and, astonishing to relate, it was the little girl of the palace. The great Gardener had kept sight of the little seed sown so long ago, and what a harvest it at last had produced!"

Miss Helm was interested in all mission fields, and was very anxious for the Woman's Foreign Missionary Society to open work in Brazil. Besides writing herself on this subject, she got Rev. J. J. Ransom, a returned missionary, to write two leaflets for her, as urgent appeals to the society and Church, for she saw away back there that it was a great opportunity for our Church, and she made strong appeals to arouse the women to en-

gage in the work. She says in one of her leaflets:
"There is in Brazil a conservative element that
sees in Protestanism the combination of intellectual
freedom and the comforts of a pure religion, and
hence the great demand for Protestant schools.
This demand must be supplied by *some* Protestant
denominations. Nowhere is our influence as a
society more sorely needed than in Brazil, where
the women are either ignorant and grossly superstitious or have been infected with the infidelity of
French literature. With such mothers, what must
the future of that country be, unless the so-much-
needed teachers from our Christian land be sent
into their midst to mold the minds and win the
hearts of the young?" She then speaks of the appropriation of the Executive Association of the society of $500 to aid the school at Piracicaba, a town
in the southern part of Brazil, and of Misses Watts
and Newman's noble work there, and later on she
speaks of an appropriation made to erect suitable
buildings for a large school. How delighted her
heart was, in the years that followed, to watch the
development of the work in that and other mission fields! After her time became fully taken up
in the great work of her life, her interest was
still strong in the cause of foreign missions. Hers
was no narrow, one-sided nature. If that judgment was ever made of her, it was false. As Dr.
Walter Lambuth said in speaking of her: "Petty
jealousy and narrowness of view were impossible

in such a nature." Her spirit lived in an atmosphere too high, too elevated for any such thing.
She used to say, "Every interest of the great
Church to which I belong is dear to me;" and she
labored under the commission, "Go ye into all
the world, and preach the gospel to every creature."
During the last years of her life, when a meeting
was held at the Methodist Publishing House in
Nashville to consider the work of establishing the
Korea Mission, although no other woman in Nashville was present, Miss Lucinda Helm was there.

Frail in body, but strong and loyal as ever in
heart, she showed great interest in the projection
of that work, and the first contribution that was
made toward it was made by *her*, a contribution
of $15. She says in one of her earnest appeals as
Editor of Leaflets in the foreign missionary work:
"Legendary lore says there was in ancient days
a saint, a pure and holy man, who, praying in his
cell, was blessed one day with a vision of his crucified Lord. As he gazed enraptured, the mon-
astery bell rang for the hour of noon. It was a
call to him to go feed the hungry and clothe the
destitute, who at that hour thronged the monas-
tery gate. He heard the call, but hesitated. How
could he leave the blessed Saviour, whose presence glorified his lonely cell? But the still small
voice within whispered, 'Do your duty!' and at
its bidding he arose, turned from the beautiful
vision, and went out to prove his love by obedi-

ence to the Master's commands. His duty faithfully performed, he returned to his cell. To his
great joy, the vision awaited him, and he heard
from the lips of his Lord this declaration: ' Hadst
thou remained, I must have gone; because thou
didst go, I have remained.' Christians, when
seeking at your Master's hand peace and joy for
your own souls; when praying in your beautiful
churches, listening with religious fervor to the
organ's notes pealing forth loud anthems of praise
to the Lamb of God, do you not hear the call:
' Go feed the hungry, clothe the naked, go preach
to the poor and those in prison?' And do you
refuse to obey the summons? You have great
joy in the hope of eternal life. You love the
Lord who has so blessed you, and would forever
dwell in his presence. ' But whoso hath this
world's good, and seeth his brother have need,
and shutteth up his bowels of compassion from
him, how dwelleth the love of God in him?'
Look at the millions of souls in heathen lands
condemned to die! The Lord commands *you* to
go teach them the way of salvation, to go bear to
them his pardon, but you heed him not. All can
not go in person, but all *can* help to send the missionary. Will you neither go nor send? Simple
and plain is the command: ' Go ye into all the
world, and preach the gospel to every creature.'
You can not fail to understand it. Clear and loud
the call is ringing; in the grandest churches above

the great organ peals, in the lowliest places of
worship, through the stillness of the closet where
you kneel to pray. You can not fail to hear it,
and truly if you obey not its summons—if you
make no effort to go forth to do your Lord's bidding, he will depart and give you the desires of
your hearts, but will send leanness into your souls."

During Miss Helm's early missionary work she
remained at " Helm Place " with her mother. An
accident rendered Mrs. Helm an invalid the last
years of her life, but as she lay upon her couch
she was still the attraction of the household as of
old. How sweet and beautiful she was in old age,
and how precious to the hearts of the beloved sisters, Miss Lucinda and Miss Mary especially, who
had made no new home ties for themselves! They
clung to her, and served her with such willing
hands and worshipful hearts! Their mother used
to say: " Queen Victoria is not better waited upon
than I am." The years of suffering left her gen-
tler and more loving to everybody and everything.
For three months before she died she was helpless, yet never a murmur escaped her. The only
wish she expressed was her last utterance, " I
want to go to my heavenly home," which prayer
was granted her on Christmas morning of 1885.

After her mother's death, Miss Lucinda, desiring
the wider opportunities furnished by a city for
Church work, went to reside with her eldest sister,
Mrs. Judge Bruce, in Louisville, Ky.

CHAPTER IV.

WOMAN'S DEPARTMENT OF CHURCH EXTENSION.

"The nerve that never relaxes, the eye that never flinches, the thought that never wanders—these are the elements of success."—Burke.

THE interests of the M. E. Church, South, were supremely dear to the heart of Miss Lucinda Helm. Unlike those who stand on the outside and do their philanthropic work independent of the Church, sneering at its coldness and formality, she believed in fighting error from the inside, and in conserving the best forces of the Church to resist the common enemy. She was not blind to its coldness, but she believed each one should do his part to make it otherwise. To her, Christ's philosophy, as embodied in his Church, is the only true philosophy of humanity; and, unless any philanthropy has as its basis and object the Christianizing of a community or people, it is worse than ill-spent, and but fosters all forms of discontent in its recipients. Therefore she believed in making all philanthropic and missionary work distinctively *Church work;* and she believed that in the Church, when it measures up to its high possibilities, there are riches in store for the world not yet dreamed of.

To this end she wrote for the Church papers, holding up the highest standards for Christian workers as Church-members. Many of her articles appeared in the *Nashville Christian Advocate* and in the *St. Louis Christian Advocate*. Through them she became known to the entire Church. Many of the bishops and other dignitaries of the Church were her stanch friends. They realized that she was not only a consecrated but a very gifted woman.

Soon after the department of Church Extension of the M. E. Church, South, was organized, in 1882, with Dr. David Morton as General Secretary, she went to him and told him she wanted to assist in that work in any way she could. He appreciated her words, and her assistance proved very valuable. She wrote in the interest of Church extension. Some of her articles were addressed to invalids, and were very touching and beautiful. In one of them she writes in the beginning of the year 1884: " I call upon you invalids, as those who abide in the inner chamber, those who are nearest and dearest to the tender heart of our Father, to continue to ask him to bless the churches we build in his name; to bless our feeble efforts to extend his kingdom in the world. I believe your prayers have ascended, and that they have aided in bringing down the rich blessings that have fallen upon the work of our Board of Church Extension, for God has

prospered it most wonderfully. I still call upon
you, as the 'shut-in builders,' to lend your aid to
this great work, to help by your prayers, your influence, and by every other way that God shall open
for you in the building of the churches, so sorely
needed in our Conferences, old and new, for in
nearly all of them are places as devoid of the benefits of Christianity as heathendom. I heard of a
man the other day in one of these neglected spots
who did not know what was meant by the word
'church.' 'Can it be so bad as that,' I said,
'and in our own midst?' Oh, how we Christians
have been wasting God's time instead of laboring
with all our strength to extend his kingdom as he
bade us do!''

In another letter to invalids she says: "Be not
weary because the activities of life have left you
stranded in a lone place. They are taken away
that nothing may hinder your heavenward gaze,
that you may nearer feel your heavenly home.
Let me tell you of a case that has come to my
knowledge through these 'letters' of mine. Then
perhaps some of you will feel as I did: humbled to
the earth with the thought that we have done
nothing, borne nothing for our Lord and Master.
I stood appalled when I read this letter. I give it
as she wrote it: 'I am one of those whom God
has shut in for nearly thirty years. Over half the
time confined to my bed, and now for more than
four years not only shut out from all means of

grace, but shut in the poorhouse. God has taken
my dear parents, brothers, and sisters, nearly all
who are dear to my heart. All are gone. I am
left in this bleak world alone, yet in the language
of Job I can say from my heart: "All the days of
my appointed time will I wait until my change
comes." If I can just be the means of doing
some good while I suffer, it is all I ask. Bless
God for my hope of heaven! Oh, happy will be
the day when we are shut in with Christ forever!
I have in my poor, weak manner prayed daily, and
almost hourly, since coming to the paupers' home,
that God would open some way of usefulness to
me, and now I hail your request as a providential
call. Please put my name on your list of "Shut-
In Builders."' This poor sister, deprived of everything but her God, in her eagerness to work
for him has been willing to take even the little
means that fell in her way for procuring the comforts and delicacies she so sorely needed. Against
this I earnestly protested as not being right, but
her desire to work for her Master knows no
bounds, and she has sent to the treasury fourteen
dollars, for some of which she has worked, although she says: 'My fingers ached and throbbed
as though an unhappy heart beat in every one of
them.' Yet she praises God that she still has the
use of her hands."

In another article, written by the distinguished
invalid, Miss Jennie Casseday, who was an inti-

mate friend of Miss Helm's, she says: "Dear shut-in sisters, did you know that in our Shut-In Band there is a branch called the Invalids' Auxiliary of Foreign Missions, and that they support missionaries, and are doing a great work for Christ? I do hope to hear of you banding yourselves together here in the South as the 'Invalids' Auxiliary to the Methodist Church Extension Work,' as our dear Miss Helm requests."

Thus through Miss Helm's articles and personal influence she became recognized as a valuable worker in Church extension, and through her correspondence in the interests of that work she enlisted many invalid women and children to contribute, although in small amounts, to the furtherance of the cause two years after the Board of Church Extension was organized. Anything that pertained to the welfare of her loved Church was of vital interest to her.

In 1885 Bishop R. K. Hargrove, while in charge of the Conferences in the West, reported to the Board of Church Extension that he had to abandon several important stations there because there was not a house to be found fit to accommodate a preacher and his family, and said: "Why could not the good women of the Church be induced to go into the work of building parsonages?" He had the year previous put the matter before the Woman's Foreign Missionary Society, and requested them to formulate some plan for building parsonages con-

nected with their work; but as they could not find
it expedient to do so, he remarked to Dr. Morton:
" It will have to be attached to Church extension." It seems from several records that Miss
Helm had a plan in her mind of this sort for the
women of the Church about the same time, and
when the matter was mentioned to her she heartily approved of it. The thought in the mind of one
of the authorities of the Church met her thought, and
in her own words she " developed the thought into
a living organization." She says afterward, in re-
ferring to that occasion: " My previous study of the
condition of our country had prepared me to be deeply impressed by the accounts given me of the efforts
our own Church was making to Christianize these
barbarous elements in the midst of our civilization.
Three thoughts took possession of me: 1. The
multitude of souls in easy reach of us dying without God or hope. 2. That God seemed to have
gathered them from every quarter of the globe
into our midst, and that we should do our part in
preaching to them the gospel of Christ. 3. That
we women of the Church ought to come to the
front and assist in providing homes for the preachers so much needed to plant the Church of Christ
in the midst of these people. I felt as if some
propelling power beyond me had entered my soul
and was moving me with an irresistible force to
throw my life into this work of helping to redeem
my country from the enemy of souls and to estab-

5

lish the kingdom of the Lord." Miss Helm was requested by the Board of Church Extension to formulate a plan including constitution and by-laws for establishing a Woman's Department of Church Extension for parsonage-building, to be submitted to the stated meeting of the Board of Church Extension held in January, 1886. She did so in a clear, businesslike manner, and her paper was by the board referred to a committee consisting of Bishop R. K. Hargrove (Chairman) and Rev. II. C. Settle and J. G. Carter, Esq. Her idea was to make provision in the constitution at that time for some phases of local home mission work, but this was strenuously opposed on the ground that it would embrace too much.

In consequence the home mission feature was abandoned for the time, and a plan for a prospective Parsonage Society reported to the board at its annual meeting in April, 1886. The report contained a memorial to the General Conference. In response the General Conference which met in May, 1886, accepted the constitution for such a department, after making a few amendments. It was incorporated as a part of the constitution of the Board of Church Extension, forming Articles XI., XII., and XIII., and reads as follows:

"Article XI. The Board of Church Extension shall organize a department known as the Woman's Department of Church Extension, the object of which shall be to collect funds by pri-

vate efforts, personal solicitations, and membership fees, donations, devises, and bequests, for
purchasing and securing parsonages. All funds
so collected shall be subject to the direction of the
General and Local Boards of Church Extension
for the object specified.

"Article XII. The officers of the Woman's Department shall be a General Secretary to be appointed by the General Board, a Secretary and
Treasurer for each Annual Conference, and a District Secretary for each presiding elder's district to
be appointed by the respective Conference Boards.

"Article XIII. The General Secretary for the
Woman's Department shall conduct the correspondence of that part of the work and furnish reports
thereof to the Secretary of the General Board.
The Secretary for each Annual Conference shall
organize Parsonage Societies in the various charges
and make reports of the work done in her Conference both to the Secretary of the Conference
Board and to the General Secretary of this department. The Treasurer for each Annual Conference shall receive the funds for the Parsonage
Societies within the Conference, of which fifty per
cent. shall be turned over to the General Board
and the other fifty per cent. remain with the Conference Board. The District Secretary shall aid
the Conference Secretary in organizing Parsonage Societies, and shall keep her informed of the
work and needs in her respective district."

One of the by-laws of the General Board reads:
" The General Secretary for the Woman's Department shall conduct the correspondence of that department, keep the Conference Secretaries supplied with information of the general work, and receive from them reports of the work done in the
Conferences. She may issue circulars, leaflets,
reports, and other publications of interest to the
work as it may require, or as the Board shall
direct."

There were also prepared at this time consti-
tutions and by-laws for the Conference Societies and the individual Parsonage Societies. Miss
Helm was appointed by the Board at once
as General Secretary of the department, and
her work grew rapidly from the very beginning.
She took hold of it, in the words of Dr. Morton,
with "remarkable intelligence, energy, and faith.
Frail of form, never knowing the blessing of good
health, and shrinking from publicity, she neverthe-
less took up a burden from which a strong man
would have shrunk, and with unfaltering steps and
a courage that was the wonder and admiration of
all who knew her she never laid it down until
God had prepared thousands of willing hands and
hearts to bear it." She was in her element when
working in conjunction and devising plans with
the master minds of the Church. Bishop Mc-
Tyeire said: " This is just what should have been
in operation years ago." From one Conference

to another Miss Helm went, organizing Parsonage Societies and inspiring the women with a zeal for the work.

Her report before the end of the first year was as follows: "In May, 1886, this new movement was determined upon and the duty devolved on the General Secretary from that time of giving to the entire Church the first information of the new work, its object and plan of operation, and to communicate with the Conference Boards and presiding elders relative to the officers to be elected by those boards. Giving this needed information of a work so entirely new required much time and unremitting thought and labor, the writing of an immense number of letters and articles for the Church papers, as well as the preparation and circulation of leaflets, etc. The Church has had within this year an opportunity to become well acquainted with the objects and plan of the work. The interest is deepening. We may say an almost universal interest in parsonages has been aroused. Those acquainted with the history of the Church say that there has never before been such a general awakening on this subject and such determination on the part of charges to provide their pastors with homes. The more difficult task follows, that of molding this interest into a substantial, lasting form in accord with the constitution of this department of Church Extension, for with it comes a large burden of local needs." She reports that

first year societies organized in 35 Conferences
and 1,595 members of the Woman's Department of
Church Extension. She says in her report for the
second year of the work ending March 31, 1888:

"The hindrances and discouragements all new
enterprises must encounter we have had to con-
tend with, yet our year's labor, by God's blessing, has borne fruit. What we have done may be
judged from the following facts: 214 societies
have been organized, reporting 3,529 members.
The children are becoming interested and are doing good work in sixty-nine places. Twenty-
three parsonages have been aided. Leaflets have
been prepared relating to the work, and 24,000
circulated. The subject has also been kept before the public through the various Church papers
and earnestly presented to individuals by personal
letters. Our efforts to secure a loan fund, put forth
only six months ago, have been so successful that
we have reason to hope we shall have a loan fund
for parsonage-building as large as that created for
church-building.

" We hear regrets on every side that this work of
parsonage-building was not begun years ago. We
hope, by God's blessing, to save the future from
the experience of the past and the regrets of the
present. We have this year at two places on the
frontier been the direct means of saving the
Church from a retreat.

"Our preachers (truly home missionaries) no

THE PREACHER'S SHELTER OF THE PAST.

A MODERN PARSONAGE.

longer labor unknown to the sympathies of their
sisters in the Eastern Conferences. Several boxes
of clothing and other necessaries have been sent
to those in want. Sabbath-school literature and
other evidences of interest have been given, which,
perhaps, may appear outside issues, yet they prove
that the thought of providing homes has taken root
in the hearts of our women and children. The
benefit that our society has proven to be to the
local work of the pastorates is shown in the report
of one hundred and seventy-one added to Sunday-schools and the sum of special donations
raised for local work amounting to $4,579.09,
independent of the regular dues of the society."

Such a report as this, at the end of the second
year's organization, of a great work done entirely
under the direction and supervision of one woman,
shows how magnificently she was endowed for
leadership. Her indomitable courage, clearness
of vision, intellectual grasp of situations, and
soundness of judgment made success imperative.
When she was not traveling in the interest of the
work, she was writing. All day long she would
use her pen, and sometimes into the night. The
literature sent out by her at this time shows not
only her earnest spirit but the broadness of the
field in which she worked and enlisted others to
work. She says in one of her leaflets:

" We have contributed largely to send the gospel to the Indians, and many of them are still in

such a state of heathenism that, as Bishop Galloway says, the sight of them ought to stir the missionary fire of the Church everywhere. We have
given as largely to other parts of the great West
where, although it be in our own country, the
heathen from every part of the globe may
be found. We have also gone into the waste
places in our old Conferences, and into the
mountains to the ignorant and needy. How
have we done this? By giving what we were assured was the most immediate and imperative
need—*homes.* Dr. John, Secretary of the Mission
Board, called the parsonage we built among the
wild tribes the ' anchor ' for our mission work in
that new field, and says of our new organization:
' It is a most important branch of missionary enterprise. No movement in our Church should command a deeper interest in the hearts of our people.'
It has been said: ' Christianize America, and the
world is saved.' Whether that be true or not, we
know that within the bounds of the great expanse
of territory we call with pride our country may be
found many representatives of nations that know
not God. How many have read of the heathen
practises among the natives of Alaska, and know
that Alaska is a part of our country—slavery of
women, infanticide, the burning of the widow on
the funeral pile or the partial burning, which is
worse still, and to which she is forced to submit,
while her shrieks are drowned by the beating of

drums, and other barbarities equal to these? One
sickens in reading the details, and wonders that
these creatures are human. But the love of Christ
can reach even such and bring them forth purified.
God help us to heed his commands! I entreat
you, my sisters, to come and help us do that which
you believe we and you should do, for the work in
our country to be done is so great that every hand
is needed to help."

In another leaflet entitled "Is Christ among
Us?" she says: "A District Secretary in Texas
writes of one of our preachers who has gone to
bed hungry one hundred nights this year. Another consecrated brother in North Mississippi,
asking for a little help to seize an opportunity to
secure a parsonage at a good bargain, says:
'My support will be very meager, and I can not
see now where it is to come from, but God knows.
The matter is with him.' He says they have
heretofore managed to live on their small salary
and keep out of debt. The terrible yearly struggle of these good men to pay rent and keep out of
debt is ruining the effectiveness of many. How
can a man study or preach as he should with such
a burden on him? We are told that one of the
ministers in North Carolina, when he reached his
circuit of eight appointments, found no house that
he could get to put his family in except a store-
house which had to be scoured, whitewashed, and
hammered until it was fit to live in, and then there

were rats enough after all that was done to almost
distract them. He says that unless the people
there are liberal it will take almost all the money
he can get to pay the rent of that store-house, and
is there any hope of his getting a parsonage?"
And thus the letters poured into Miss Helm's office
from all quarters—the Indian Mission, Montana,
Oregon, California, and all of the Southern states.
Some of them were full of gratitude for what the
Woman's Parsonage Society had done for them,
and others were making earnest appeals for help.
She wrote to all of them, and where she could not
furnish help she encouraged these heroic men
and their families by her strong Christian spirit
and faith.

In all her explanatory leaflets and articles, and
in her plans for the establishment of new departments of the work she wrote with clearness, ac-
curacy, and complete mastery of the subject equal
to a jurist. Discouragements were frequently presented, but she was determined not to heed them.
She says: "We know a movement with an object like ours can not be stopped. God will see to
that. But we are restive under the fact that it
moves more slowly than it should, because of the
inactivity of those who should most vigorously push
it on. If it were some general principle at stake,
one might bear this with more equanimity, feeling
that God will ultimately cause the right to prevail.
But it is not that. It is little children suffering,

weary mothers worn with toil, and husbands and
fathers going about doing good with heavy hearts,
not only for the privations they must bear but because of the burdens resting upon their families—
burdens they are unable to remove, because their
time is given to God's work. I can not calmly say:
'All shall be well some time.' I can not wait for the
future. I must relieve my poor, tired, heart-break-
ing sister yonder, before she gives down under the
weight of daily care. I want to lift the burden off
of *that* godly brother—that very one (not some
future one I know not of), that he may do with a
free heart and untrammeled mind the work of the
Master. Faith tells me that God has heard their
prayers and is urging us on to be his means of answering them. 'But why,' ask those who carp—
'why are men and their families sent to such
places where they must suffer?' Why are they
sent? Why is the gospel sent *anywhere?* Why
have missionaries gone to foreign fields to be
slaughtered? They go in obedience to the voice
of Almighty God that in trumpet tones has pro-
claimed the command: 'Go ye into all the world,
and preach the gospel to every creature!' They
go because the Spirit of God will not let them stay.
It is the grand policy of the Methodist Church to
send the gospel wherever there is need for it, and
our consecrated ministers go wherever they are
sent, though they may know it involves suffering
for them and theirs. With silent heroism they

have endured for Christ's sake hardships that develop noble characters. But away with the sentiment that applauds this nobility and does not re-
flect upon the attitude of those who can and do
not relieve these oppressed ones.' As their trials
exalt them, our permitting such trials lowers us."

At the close of the third year of the Woman's
Department of Church Extension she says:

" During the past year we have proved, we
sincerely hope, the far-seeing wisdom of the words
of our prince of bishops, McTyeire. He said to
to the Conferences over which he presided:
'Brethren, there is nothing before you more important.' Never shall I forget the bright expression of pleasure on his face, nor his words of
commendation about our work. They have been
as a cordial in moments of weakness. The women
of other denominations are awake and abroad in
the land, pressing forward, extending the influence
and bounds of Christianity as represented by their
respective Churches.

"Our society projects no work, sends no missionaries, but follows in the wake of every forward
movement made by our Church. Our work is to
build up, establish, and put upon a sure footing
each post. The good we have accomplished this
year has opened the eyes of our people to see as
never before how the power of the Church to advance will be greatly increased by having a well-
organized parsonage-building society. Eighty-one

thousand one hundred leaflets of such a character as to be desired by other denominations have been freely distributed by our Secretaries, and we trust will be productive of great good. The total number of members at the close of this year is five thousand eight hundred and twenty-one, and the total amount raised by the Woman's Department for general and local work $9,607.25. There are also one hundred and forty-five names on the Preachers' Wives' Loan Fund, and many other indications of increasing interest in new features of the work.''

In the fourth and last year of the society, under the limited title ' Woman's Department of Church Extension,' the increase in dues over the preceding year was $600, the membership at the close of this first quadrennium was seven thousand two hundred and sixteen, and the amount of money raised for general and local work $14,554.31. This work during these four years was represented in thirty-six Conferences of the Southern Methodist Church, and more than seven thousand women were working together through Conference Societies and individual auxiliaries to establish homes for the itinerant ministry in the South, Southeast, and West. But the responsibility devolving entirely, as it did, upon one individual was great, and the extreme pressure would have been unbearable many times had it not been for her indomitable courage and sublime faith. She realized that in

the projection of this work she stood too much
alone, although that realization never inclined her
to withdraw her energies. Upon her devolved the
duty of giving to the whole Church information of
the work. Many emergencies and contingencies
that could not be foreseen necessarily arose in
this untried field, the responsibility of meeting them
was great, and required wisdom and strength to be
gained only from the divine Source. A suitable
literature had to be prepared and every detail of
the work provided for. Thousands of letters and
postals were written. At the same time the subject
was kept continually before the Church at large
through the Church papers; leaflets, programs,
and blanks were made ready each quarter in time,
neglecting no minutiæ that would render interesting the monthly meetings of both adult and juvenile auxiliaries. Quarterly and annual reports were
also promptly and carefully prepared. In the inauguration of the work a certain amount of traveling had to be done by some one, but there was no
one save the Secretary who, though shrinking from
that ordeal, visited eleven Conferences ranging
from Indian Mission to North Carolina. The office work that accumulated during her absence was
met unaided. Only a few days during the entire
time did she receive clerical assistance. It was
the work of several officers and committees devolving upon one individual. Yet she gave her entire
time, strength, heart, and soul for its success.

The Board of Church Extension desired to appropriate to her a salary of $600 a year, but she refused to receive it. Dr. Morton urged her to take it, and said: "It is a debt, and when you die it can be collected." The only reply she made to this was to add a statement to her will which released the board from any indebtedness to her. She was so determined in this matter because some complaints had come to her ears about the payment of salaries. Then, too, the collections of the Woman's Department were so small she said it would look as if she were working for financial benefit.

Her desire was to give everything, even "all her living," to the Lord. To every call made by the Church she responded wherever it was possible, saying: "I meant what I said when I promised to support the institutions of the Church." When she published her little book "Gerard" she gave the Church Extension Society the first proceeds, saying: "I want to render to God the first-fruits of all I make."

At the close of the first quadrennium she had been brought, through her extensive correspondence and personal work, in touch with the entire field of crying need in all sections of the South and West; and, while her watchword was, "A parsonage in every charge!" she felt a burning desire to furnish more than a parsonage as she saw all that was thrown open to her gaze. Her articles and leaflets written at this time distinctly

show that nothing less than the fullest and com-
pletest organized effort for *home missions* could
satisfy her. She thought out new plans and
prayed over them, and was determined to work
for the enlargement of the charter of the society. Everywhere she went, and upon all sides, her
ears were filled with cries for help. The poor,
the ignorant, the destitute, the depraved, the city
waifs, mountain whites, negroes, Chinese, and Japanese were making loud appeals, by their very
existence, to the great mother heart of this woman.

Although she knew from her past experience
that obstacles and objections would be numerous
on every hand in the broadening of her work to
such unlimited bounds, she was now determined
not to relinquish the plan. When she became
convinced that it was an imperative need, and approved of by her Lord, she knew no such thing
as fear. "This is our Father's work," she said.
"He has given our Church money and Christian
workers: what is man that he should oppose God!"
She wept and prayed alone with God. She had
given her means and her all, unreservedly, to him:
what should opposition signify? He would make
her work a success: what did the constant and
life-long feebleness and pain of her body signify? She shut her ears to its cries. Her physical
weakness was extreme, but that did not stay her
nor induce her to stand and wait. Many a time
she had to be propped up in her bed all night, with

ice packed to her heart. When astonishment was expressed at this, she said: "It is my one slim chance to live, and I am going to live." "Why do you not stop such heavy work?" inquired her physician and friends. "You will kill yourself." "I know how frail I am," she replied, "but my frailty shall honor Jesus." Surely she realized the truth of the great apostle's words: "When I I am weak, then am I strong." As Dr. II. C. Morrison has said of her, "never in the history of our Church has a great brain sustained by so frail a body accomplished through arduous toil such a work, and like the immortal Watts she will live forever in the great heart of the Church."

CHAPTER V.

"All great work is at first impossible."—Carlyle.

IT was Miss Helm's determination to make a plea at the General Conference of 1890, through the Board of Church Extension, for the enlargement of the charter for woman's work. Her plan was that, without detaching the name " Parsonage," this organization embrace other forms of home mission work; and while the work of building parsonages should still remain under the supervision of the Board of Church Extension, all other branches of the work should become independent of that board and come under the management of a Central Committee composed of competent women.

She presented her plans for the extension of the work to some of the Church authorities before the General Conference of 1890 convened, but even her stanchest friends thought it an unwise plan, attended with great risks. Again and again she went to Dr. Morton and some of the bishops, trying to show the imperative needs in our Church for a connectional organization known distinctively as home missions; but the objection was presented that the Church was not ready for such an

organization. She was told that the Parsonage
Society had hardly gotten a sure footing in the
Church at that time, and by moving too fast, and
undertaking to enlarge the work to such an extent,
she would find it impracticable and calculated to
do more harm than good. She insisted that it
would not interfere with the parsonage work.
She had found in her efforts to establish parsonage societies that the women of the Church were
organized into all sorts of other societies; such as,
" Ladies' Aids," " Pastors' Aids," " Dorcas's,"
" Sewing Society," " Social Society," " Young
Ladies' Aids," all of which were doing *home mission* work in their own churches, and many were
doing interdenominational work also. The wom-
en in many churches were supplying mere philanthropic societies with the means to do the very
things the Church is called to do, and, upon the
ground that their entire time and means were absorbed in these things, they objected to the Parsonage Society.

As she had visited the different Conferences
she had observed that some of the women of the
Church were awake to the needs of established
organized home mission work for the M. E.
Church, South. Here and there expressions to
this effect were reported to her. In the state
of Georgia an appeal had been made to the
women of that state to unite in forming in every
Methodist church in Georgia a woman's *Home*

Missionary Society. The appeal was strong, and signed by three of the most influential women of the Church. It had, however, met with little response or encouragement from the women or the pastors, and, consequently, had proved unsuccessful. Miss Helm's position was that if "home missions" was incorporated in the work of the new organization for parsonage-building and endorsed by the General Conference, all local church societies would become merged into that department of the organization, and thus do away with the objectionable number of societies. The charities of the church would be condensed and due credit allowed for the work being done by its members. Moreover, the women of the Church would by means of the proposed plan become larger in purpose, heart, and work in learning the needs of the entire country. The objection was then made that, if there was a drain on the sympathies and pocket-books of the people for *home missions,* it would cripple the work of *foreign missions.* This objection Miss Helm refuted as wholly illogical and unwarranted by examples given of home and foreign mission societies cooperating successfully in other denominations. She wrote articles on the subject, and conducted a large correspondence, presenting the matter to the influential women as well as to the men of the Church.

Bishop McTyeire said to Mrs. E. E. Wiley, in speaking of the work: "Have you ever met Lu-

cinda Helm?'' She replied: '' No, I only know
of her.'' '' Well,'' said the Bishop, with that
peculiar, quizzical look of his through half-closed
lids, '' she is as keen as a brier. She is all brains.
You ought to know her.'' Mrs. Wiley was then
absorbed in the interest of foreign missions, and
she became eager to understand the secret of Miss
Helm's innovation. After she became acquainted
with her and her great projects for the Church,
she said: '' Miss Helm seems to me in her deduc-
tive trend of mind to be in the center of a plan of
mighty work for the Church, and from her frail
fingers there goes out an electric current of spiritual power to its farthest periphery. I never
knew any one to struggle through such difficulties
under such untoward circumstances as she in her
unselfish devotion to a cause in which she finds
comparatively but little sympathy. To those of
us on the outside the prospect of accomplishing
what she proposed was as the frazzled edges of a
forlorn hope. The Conferences did not seem to
understand the work she proposed to do, the body
of the womanhood of the Church was committed
to foreign missions, and any' thing that looked like
a disturbance of the settled autonomy of the
Church elicited a frown from the ' powers that
be.' But *her* keen eyes discerned where the
walls of her beloved Zion were weakening, and she
started with her bricks and mortar to the faithful
workmen.''

Her letters, powerful like Paul's, went to hundreds of representative women and to the ministry as well; but although some of them were largely in favor of her plans, there was but little sympathy manifested by the body of women as a whole, while many of the ministers throughout the Church were opposed to her plan, and even sent in appeals to the Board of Church Extension to "kill the new movement." Scores of them had objected to the Parsonage Society in the beginning; and now after that had gained a foothold, notwithstanding their protests, they objected to the enlargement of the work on the ground that if the needs of our country in every direction became known to the women of the Church, there would not be as much done for the building of parsonages. Miss Helm was assured that it would *increase* instead of *diminish* that department, as well as every other department of Church work; and thus through months of vigorous appeal and agitation she stood bravely to her self-imposed task, until many of the women of the Church were brought up to her own high conception of the duty before them and how to meet it.

Like a seed that sprouts from under the edge of some great boulder, the work would not "down." Women of influence began to stand shoulder to shoulder with their standard-bearer, and to realize with her what a broadening and deepening influence the proposed work might become to the

Church. She was ever the pastor's earnest friend, although some pastors were too blind to see it. She says in one of her appeals:

"Our work does not end with the building of parsonages. That should be only a part of it, although a very important part, but further, our desire is to organize around each pastor a society of faithful women filled with a zealous determination to do their part to bring their country to Christ.

"Our constitution is founded on the commission, 'Preach the gospel to every creature.' There is power in united effort. If we can enlist the women to undertake home mission enterprises, and then unite all their work, local and otherwise, under one great connectional organization with many branches, it will give not only definite shape and regularity but overwhelming *power* to our efforts, and we shall see far greater results in every line than at present. The policy of the Methodist Church is connectional, and far more good may be accomplished in conforming to this policy than in going contrary to it. Many of us are determined to do home missionary work. How can we willingly shut our eyes any longer to the palpable needs everywhere about us?

"When it is known that in the one state of Kentucky (and it is not behind others) there were at the time our Board of Church Extension was organized thirteen counties without a church of any

denomination, can we wonder that in these church-
less regions the densest ignorance prevails? It is
told by one who visited those mountain regions
that a dying woman, when spoken to of Christ,
looked at the speaker in surprise, and, raising herself up a little, asked: "Did he come before or
after the war?" Such accounts more often cause
laughter among Christians than the realization that
such words as given by that dying woman are an
accusation against them before the Judge of all the
earth. The chaplains in penitentiaries through
those regions say: 'Ignorance, poverty, and
whisky have made ninety-five hundredths of our
convicts.' These mountain people are not so vi-
cious as ignorant, and the forces of evil are continually present. Then let us glance at our Western
territory. Every one knows that there are places
to be found from which primeval darkness and
heathenism have never been driven, and the influx
of the Chinese with their idols and foul customs is
so great as to alarm the government. How few,
comparatively, of our people go into foreign fields;
but see the thousands upon thousands of Christians
here at home. God is distributing these idol-wor-
shiping Chinese as servants in Christian homes,
and thousands are brought within easy reach of
our churches, to which we may take them. God
acts in no uncertain way. What he says in
Scripture he speaks also in the strong, unmista-
kable language of facts, as the records of history

show. Not only do those at a distance need our home mission work, but it is equally needed right at our doors. Do you see that poor, little outcast crouching in the alley-corner because he has no home, driven to vice by misery? Do you see that poor, degraded woman, whose heart often throbs with the agony of remorse and despair in the midst of her guilt? Do you see that criminal in his cell, embittered toward the world because not a soul in it cares for him? These are God's creatures. Have you no care for them, and yet profess to be God's child? As members of the Methodist Church should not we do missionary work *everywhere* among the godless inhabitants of this land, and patiently labor and teach them the way of salvation?

" This work can not be done in a day, neither can it be done by spasmodic, irregular effort, but can be accomplished only by united, concentrated, tireless effort of the Church."

Thus, in this appeal through one of her early leaflets, we observe that she hoped for the most mature development of home mission work in our Church. One of her earnest coworkers, Mrs. J. D. Hammond, wrote an article on the work at this time which was afterward printed in leaflet form and widely circulated. In it she says: " There are those among us who oppose this society because they fear it will interfere with other Church work. Even the women, sometimes forgetting their righteous indignation when some of the fathers and brethren in At-

lanta opposed the Woman's Foreign Missionary
Society on that same ground, look askance at this
youngest daughter of the Church and wonder
what the child is coming to with such lungs! It
would seem that this comes from looking at the
matter upside down or crosswise or sidewise or
somewise that is not square in the face. The
Church's business is to save the world. The
work is one work, and it can no more be prospered
in foreign lands by stopping the work at home,
than one's left hand can be prospered by tying
up the right until it is paralyzed. Will it prosper China or Brazil to let the floods of ungodli-
ness gather in our Western country till they sweep
away our outposts and rise in threatening power
around our Eastern citadel? Is it good strategy, is
it common sense, while throwing our forces over
into China, to leave in between our advance-guard
and the main body a vast region in possession of
the enemy? May God forgive us for trifling with
this matter as we have heretofore done."

Miss Helm had published "A Warning," by
Dr. Y. J. Allen, one of our greatest missionaries
to foreign lands. In it he says: "If we value our
Christianity at home and our efforts among the
heathen in foreign lands, we should no longer
close our eyes to the vital importance of the contest between Christianity and heathendom on our
western coast, now attracting the eyes of the
world. It is to the Church, and not to the civil

government, that we must look for power to meet this issue as Christians should. According to the Word of God there is but one way to meet it: the Church must bring these heathen nations in their own land to Christ." So forceful were the answers made to all objections, and so earnest the appeals, that many changed their views and began to see the urgent need for a woman's *home mission* organization in the Church. Great was the rejoicing among them when at the General Conference of 1890 the seal of approval was conclusively given, largely through the personal intercession of Dr. H. C. Morrison, who was that year Chairman of the Committee on Church Extension, and the Parsonage and Home Mission Society was officially recognized as one of the connectional benevolences of the Methodist Episcopal Church, South. The following names were then proposed as constituting the Central Committee of this society, and they were adopted by the board: Mrs. E. E. Wiley, President; Miss Lucinda B. Helm, General Secretary; Mrs. George P. Kendrick, General Treasurer. Managers: Mrs. R. K. Hargrove, Mrs. Nathan Scarritt, Mrs. D. Atkins, Mrs. S. S. King, Miss Emily M. Allen, Mrs. Maria Carter, Mrs. Ellen Burdette, Mrs. John Carter, and Miss Belle Bennett. Shortly afterward Miss Bennett was obliged to resign, as she was agent for the Scarritt Bible and Training School, and the pressure of work in both became too great.

Her sister, Miss Sue Bennett, was elected in her
place, and after her death Miss Belle became a
permanent member of the Central Committee.
Besides these twelve names, the name of Mrs.
Gross Alexander was added as Editor of Leaflets.
Thus the great responsibilities of this work became divided among a number of women, and
Miss Helm had the wise counsel of those who became her earnest and devoted coworkers and
friends. The family of Mr. George P. Kendrick,
who have an inheritance of devotion to the Church,
rendered the most loving and faithful assistance to
Miss Helm from the beginning. A room in their
beautiful home was consecrated to Church work,
and Miss Helm was ever a welcome guest there.
Every development of the new organization was
encouraged by the members of this Christian family. The Board of Church Extension had no supervision of the work done by the Central Committee
under the head of "Home Missions." The funds
appropriated to parsonages, however, have from
the beginning passed through that board, it acting
as trustee of the society in all matters of legacies,
holdings of real estate, and the administration of
parsonage loan funds.

In the fifth annual report of the woman's organization, which is the first of the Woman's Parsonage and Home Mission Society, Miss Helm says:
"The first annual meeting of the Central Committee was held in Chestnut Street Methodist

Church, at Louisville, April 9-11, 1891. . . .
Reports show improvement all along the line.
Ninety auxiliaries were added during the year.
A permanent loan fund of $3,000 is on hand.
The increase in dues this year has amounted to
$139.94. The Central Committee determined not
to lessen its efforts to secure parsonages, which it
deems a very important feature of our home mission work, but to stress more than heretofore
other forms of home mission work also. These
women have already created a wide-spread interest and collected large funds to meet the demands,
but the work to be done is great. If our country
is to be brought to Christ, there must be no idlers
in Zion. We have been encouraged this year by
the manifestation of larger interest among the
women of the Church than ever before. The
added title of 'Home Missions' to the society has
interfered with no other enterprise, and has contributed greatly to the awakening of a more general interest in every line of Church work. Much
credit is due to the President, Mrs. Wiley, who,
during the last six months, has traveled a great
number of miles and visited many of the Conferences in the interests of the society. She arouses
enthusiasm wherever she goes."

Mrs. Wiley says of her work at this time: "As
I journeyed through the Conferences, Miss Helm's
letters and prayers followed me. Sometimes my
way was hedged about, and instead of friends I

found and felt sharp arrows of the Mighty, with
coals of Juniper! But her hand never left my
pulse-beat, and her faith and love were to me as
the oil of healing when the wound was sorest. I
learned to lean on her. I forgot how frail she
was. I thought her a Gibraltar. It was a source
of refreshing surprise to me to note the breadth of
the woman as she stood in the center of her great
plan appropriating the inflowing elements of success. No matter how various their forms, each
had its place and part. If her judgment differed
from that of others, she never failed to recognize
and appropriate whatever of merit there was in the
plans of others, and her counsel was so manifestly
of the Lord that all felt its force. She was divine-
ly fitted for this work.''

A leaflet was published about this time giving
Bishop Hendrix's views of the work under the en-
larged charter, and reading thus: "A modest
pamphlet entitled ' The Fifth Annual Report of the
Woman's Work' (the first of the Woman's Parsonage and Home Mission Society), is on my table
and sets me to thinking. It is the development of
an idea in a good woman's brain to provide homes
for our preachers, and in that limited form has
borne fruit in many a charge that would still be
without a parsonage save for this society. It has
helped to establish the work of the Church in
many places, and by enlisting more than seven
thousand women and children to work for others

has done much to develop their Christian lives.
No other Church of which we have knowledge has
been so favored. But worthy as is this specific
work, the time has come, in the judgment of the last
General Conference, to enlarge the operations of the
Parsonage Society by adding to it the work of
home missions in general. This will connection-
alize all the hitherto local societies, which now,
though doing no less in their own fields, will be
prepared to aid in the general work as well.
Every pastor who has a Pastor's Aid Society will
find it wise to have it become an auxiliary of this
general society, as helping to quicken the zeal of
its members and to increase their efficiency in
Church work even of a purely local character.
Not only will it result in the building and equip-
ment of many parsonages and in the building
up of many Sunday-schools and congregations
by looking after the youth and the strangers, but
in more earnest study of the Bible and in greater
aptness in soul-winning. What an amount of work
for the Master is possible for the Marys and Mar-
thas and Salomes of our day if intelligently organized and directed! Within the limits of our
Church are four cities of a population of 200,000
souls, three others with a population of more than
100,000, seven others with a population of over
50,000, and twenty-two containing more than 20,-
000. In all of these cities we have a mission as a
Church. Women missionaries should be employed

especially trained for the work to be done. Mr.
Wesley understood the great service which such
noble women as Hester Ann Rogers, Mrs. Fletch-
er, and others could do wisely, and availed himself
of and directed their labors. May we not hope
for a new era in our beloved Church as we see our
noble women becoming diligent in such labors?
May there not be a larger number who can and
will devote their entire time to this work? Without Lydia could Paul have planted the church in
Philippi?"

During this year of 1891 the "Angel Band
Loan Fund" was established by Miss Sue Ben-
nett, although the name was given by Miss Helm.
Twenty-one were recorded as members by the
payment of $20, one of which was the name of
Mrs. Helm, made by Miss Lucinda.

She says, in speaking of these loan funds: "We
are authorized to raise other loan funds also, such
as 'Named Loan Funds,' the donor or donors
having the privilege of naming the fund, thus
erecting a monument of good deeds to bear the
name of the one honored." All the money donated in loan funds was to be used exclusively for
parsonage-building. This was also the first year
in which a Conference Organizer was elected—
Mrs. Poynter, of the Kentucky Conference—and
great interest was exhibited for extending the
work in the mountains of Kentucky.

At the close of the next fiscal year, ending

March, 1892, Miss Helm writes: "The places to which grants and loans were made for parsonages were scattered over fourteen states and territories this year, and the work of the Central Committee was highly commended by the Board of Church Extension. The Central Committee and the Conferences and auxiliaries together helped one hundred and thirty-five parsonages (more than two and one-half a week), to the amount of more than $14,000. This far exceeds our report in any previous year in this department of the work. During these six years since the organization of the woman's society more parsonages have been built than in all the first fifty years of Methodism. Not only have homes been provided, but boxes of supplies and personal gifts been sent to supplement meager salaries."

In speaking of the publications of the society for the year, she says: "More than fifty thousand excellent leaflets have been sent out by our editor, and the paper which is the official organ of the society, *Our Homes*, the first number of which appeared in January of this year, has already been put upon a paying basis."

The subject of the evangelization of the mountain people of Kentucky attracted much attention at the meeting of the Central Committee, and we determined during this coming year to endeavor to raise funds for a mission in those mountains to be known as the "Sue Bennett Memorial." Miss

Sue Bennett, as Secretary of the Kentucky Conference Society, was planning the mission when our Father called her home. Miss Belle Bennett subscribed to this mission $500.

Miss Helm adds, in regard to the large fields of work before the society: "In viewing the work that has been accomplished we should consider the great field of labor in our large cities calling for the zeal and patience of consecrated Christian workers. We should have in all our cities trained Bible women, and, also, *industrial schools with modern plans for Christian workers* among neglected children."

The next year her seventh annual report shows a decided if not a great advance. The increase of dues amounted to $936, and the grand total of funds raised by the entire society for all purposes showed an *increase* over the preceding year of $14,183.69.

Experience each year demonstrated the fact that the amount given to help parsonages stimulated the people so helped to raise themselves double the amount granted them by the society. As an illustration of this, one woman in the Northwest writes: "In giving the subject much thought I have concluded that the Woman's Parsonage and Home Mission Society gives us the easiest and most complete solution of the question: 'How can we become self-sustaining?' In our work on Oakland Circuit the $200 granted us by the Central Committee has enabled us to raise a $600 subscription for building, and we will have, when finished, a beautiful little home worth $1,000. Yet without aid from the society we could not have done anything, but through the help and inspiration of the society our subscription has come not only from our own people but from others outside."

Notwithstanding the phenomenal success of the work, Miss Helm sometimes received very discouraging letters from the brethren, written in a fault-finding and dictatorial spirit; but she bore this with an extraordinary Christian grace. Upon one of these occasions she wrote to the President, Mrs. Wiley: "The brethren do not understand. They do not want us to help them, but I feel the Church is losing vantage-ground for lack of parsonages, and that hurts me. We *must* help them." Never was there a plea made to her from a homeless preacher's wife that failed to bring her to her closet in prayer, and prayer invariably reassured her and unburdened her trusting heart.

At one time she accompanied Mrs. Burdette to a meeting of the Kentucky Conference, and upon their arrival appearances indicated a complete failure. There were but seven or eight women present. She said, after viewing the situation: "Let us go tell Jesus all about it, and get his help." She arose from her knees strengthened and encouraged. Like a little child whose troubles are instantly forgotten by a parent's caress, her

spirit was reassured and rejoicing after coming, if
only for a moment, into her Heavenly Father's
presence. They went to work urging the women
to attend the meeting. They talked and planned
and prayed until after two o'clock that night, and
the next day they had a large audience. She
would surmount obstacles and overcome difficulties.

In her seventh annual report she says concerning the work specified under the head of "Home
Missions:" "This year our school in the mountains of Kentucky has become a fact. Seven
thousand five hundred dollars has been raised in
the Kentucky Conference for the school, a beautiful site donated, and the work of building will
soon begin. It is to be an educational base
from which our trained workers may go out as
teachers among the poor and those without God
through the mountain districts. We need also to
undertake as a branch of our work *Methodist
missions* in the *evangelization* of our *cities*. We
should, as women of the Church, stop scattering
our forces in little detachments here and there
and serving as volunteers in the forces of other
Churches or philanthropies, and firmly unite and
cooperate with our pastors, going forward under
the authority of our own beloved Church to do
this great work."

In this seventh year was held the first convention of the Parsonage and Home Mission Society.

It convened at St. Louis, in St. John's Church, May 9, 1893, and lasted two days and evenings, Bishop Hargrove presiding. This convention was to be the test of how the organization would be received by the Church, and Miss Helm worked and prayed earnestly for its success. Those who had promised to take part in the program failed her at the last, and, in her own words, she "threw the whole matter over on God and trusted him for its success." Bishop Duncan made an address the first evening, showing the benefits accruing to the Church from good parsonages. Bishop Fitzgerald spoke, and awakened much interest in a mission for the Cubans. Dr. Allen, of China, spoke in the afternoon, showing how the work done in this country for the salvation of souls encouraged missionaries in foreign lands. Dr. Walter Lambuth awakened intense interest by his address on "City Evangelization." When Miss Helm saw the continued interest manifested all through the crowded house, and heard the charming words of these men and Dr. Mathews, Dr. Messick, and others heartily endorsing the Woman's Parsonage and Home Mission Society, she arose, and, although ever shrinking from public gaze, forgot herself, forgot her labors of mind and body. Her weak voice grew strong, her face lit up, and, as in elegant English the words flowed from her lips, many present felt that the Spirit of God was upon her, and loud "Amens" were heard all over the room.

With rising votes the women determined to unite all their local societies in the future under this connectional organization, and make a force strong enough to plan largely for Christ in the cities within the bounds of the Methodist Episcopal Church, South. It was a most successful convention from beginning to end, and the originator of it all said at the close, with beaming eyes: "God has answered our prayers. Our convention is a great success." It marked an epoch in the history of the society.

Although this seventh year was largely in advance of any preceding one in the history of the society, Miss Helm's family and friends saw plainly that the extreme pressure on her of editing without assistance the paper, and doing the work and extensive correspondence of General Secretary besides, was fast breaking down her delicate constitution, and could not possibly continue much longer. She told us one day how she had to be carried to her sister's home, and was so ill for a time that no one thought she could possibly recover, yet she herself was confident that was not to be the end. "Well, for the sake of the work," we said, "if for no other consideration, will you not give up a part of it?" "If Mrs. Nathan Scarritt will be General Secretary," she replied, "I will resign; but I do not want any one else, and I know my Father is not going to take me home until that place, as well as some others, is properly filled.

Mrs. Scarritt, having the matter repeatedly put before her by Miss Helm, was finally induced to accept the office of General Secretary, which she did at a called meeting of the Central Committee October 11, 1893. As Miss Helm retired from office she closed her annual report with the following words: "Without a dissenting voice the choice of the Central Committee, and the society at large as far as could be heard from, was Mrs. Nathan Scarritt as General Secretary upon our resignation. We give this part of our work into the hands of another as a mother trusts her child to the guidance of another with clinging love but intense gratitude to God for preparing one so worthy to take charge of it. She is preeminently fitted to carry out the aims of the society, to inspire the women of the Church we love with a deeper love for souls and a vital interest in the salvation of our country. God be with you all!"

CHAPTER VI.

FULL DEVELOPMENT OF THE WORK.

"There is nothing so singular in life as this: that every opposition appears to lose its substance when one actually grapples with it."—Hawthorne.

A S the result of the persistent and determined efforts of Miss Helm and her coworkers year after year this great home mission organization is to-day one of the most potent factors for the extension of the kingdom of God in the entire Church. She saw with prophetic vision five years ago, when she resigned as General Secretary, the entire structure as it now stands, and realized that it would require the incarnation of other lives besides her own to bring it to its fullest proportions. She therefore rendered unremitting assistance to the workers in their various fields while she poured the strength of her remaining life into her paper, which proved to be a constant stimulus in the advance of the work. The society is now firmly established, and with a membership of twenty thousand is doing much to help the needy and sorrowing in our South and West land. The day of beginnings is past, and plans are being devised for extensive work in the future. In the place of one peerless woman standing alone ready to offer her life for this cause there are now hundreds of women giving their time, talents, and means for its advancement.

The educational department is established on a firm basis. A magnificent school-building at London, Ky., for mountain boys and girls has been recently finished, and the property is valued at $20,-000. The society also owns a handsome school-building at Tampa, Fla., for Cubans, worth $7,000; an industrial school and home for orphans at Greeneville, Tenn., valued at $7,000; and a rescue home at Dallas, Tex., which when finished will be worth $15,000. The Sue Bennett Memorial School, at London, Ky., is, although in its infancy, one of the leading institutions in the entire mountain region of Kentucky. This specific work was inaugurated chiefly through the efforts of Miss Sue Bennett; and, that her memory might be revered by those benefited in the institution, it was named after her.

The Superintendent of Mountain Work, Miss Belle Bennett, who is now also President of the society, says in regard to this school: " In February, 1896, the Board of Managers appointed by the Central Committee for the projected training-school at London, Ky., had a called meeting and ordered the work of building to begin. A splendid site, with twenty-two acres of land for campus, was purchased, and on June 25 the corner-stone was laid by Bishop E. R. Hendrix in the presence

of a large assemblage of deeply interested people.
The work was pushed forward until late in the fall,
with the hope of completing the building in time
for occupancy in January, 1897. But the strin-
gency of the times rendering this impossible, it was
decided early in December to open the school in
the old school-building of the town. Prof. J. C.
Lewis, recently of Ogden College, was chosen
Principal. On January 5, 1897, with a faculty of
three teachers, the school was opened with nearly
one hundred pupils in attendance. The number
continued to increase until a fourth teacher became
a necessity. Nearly or quite one-third of the students are public school teachers representing five
or six of the mountain counties. These young men
and women in their little schools in the future will
come in contact with the people whom, up to this
time, the Church has practically failed to reach.
A special normal course will be given during the
months of April and May. God has opened in
this school a wide and effectual door through
which the gospel of redemption may be preached
to a much-neglected people." The large building
has recently been finished, and the school is in
operation there. It was a source of great disap-
pointment to Miss Helm that she was prevented
from being present at the dedication of this building. In a letter, written in September, 1897, to Mrs.
Sawyer she said: " That school has always been
so close to my heart, and it is a comfort inexpress-

ible to see it complete and a success before I go my way."

The Industrial Home and School, at Greeneville, Tenn., was opened in August, 1896, and is under the auspices of the Woman's Parsonage and Home Mission Society of the Holston Conference. It owes its existence and success largely to the indefatigable and enthusiastic leadership and labors of our former President, Mrs. E. E. Wiley.

The property, consisting of a handsome new building of thirteen rooms and about sixty acres of land, was bought for $7,000. The farm produces supplies for table and stock. Four superior Christian women have the house in charge, including the care and education of the children, who are taken from the ages of eighteen months to nine years.

Mrs. Wiley writes concerning it: "Ours is not an 'institution.' It is a 'home' in all its appointments. The children have forgotten that they were poor and friendless. They sit at the table and are served as our own children. There will be no difference between this home and the best to which we shall commit them later. Demands for our children are coming in, and we shall put some in homes we select. Ten have already been put into good homes, and the names of thirty children are now enrolled. The girls are taught to sew, cook, and keep house generally. The boys do all outside work on the farm, and in-

side work when needed.   The larger children attend church and are trying to be honest, earnest
Christians.   The outlook on the whole is good.
Most of the children are easily led and quick to
learn.   We have no salaried women, maid or mis-
tress.   All service is freely given in this home.
The plan first agreed upon we have decided to
change somewhat.   There is great need for a
school for girls from twelve to eighteen years old
in our mountain population.   They should be
taught 'how the other half lives,' and so from
this plant we hope to establish helping schools for
the mothers and daughters hid away among the
hills.   This can be done with but little outlay of
money if wisely managed, and the talents needed
are rusting in our cultured homes.   Prayer, faith,
work, and hard sense will remove the mountains
for us."

These are the beginnings of the work of this organization for the mountain people.   The hope is
to assist the Church to establish in the years to
come educational centers in the entire southeastern
mountain territory.   There is no nobler work un-
dertaken by the Church anywhere than the opening of civilization to these hungry-hearted mountain people.   Some important and interesting facts
regarding them and the section of country in which
they live are given in an article by our President,
Miss Belle Bennett, from which we quote the following:

INDUSTRIAL HOME AND SCHOOL, GREENEVILLE, TENN.

8

"Scientists tell us that heredity and environment are the master influences of the organic world; that these have made all of us what we are, and that these remain the great natural forces which 'shape our lives.' Accepting this as true, let us look for a moment at the people and conditions of life in these mountain parts of our country, and learn, if we can, what it is that makes this mission ground, and places a peculiar obligation upon every individual Christian and conscientious citizen.

"In the last few years several learned gentlemen have written voluminously to prove that these people who now live in the southeastern portion of Kentucky, in those counties that are distinctively mountainous, and also in that part of West Virginia immediately bordering on them, are not a people having the same ancestry and the same blood as those who live in the blue-grass region of Kentucky and in the Shenandoah Valley of Virginia. These gentlemen prove quite conclusively to themselves that these 'poor mountain whites,' as they are called, 'are the descendants of that destitute and semi-criminal class who were sold into service to pay their fines and the cost of their transportation into the colonies;' or, so many of their names beginning with Mc., they get their descent direct from the Scotch-Irish element that located in the Blue Ridge counties, moving back as the number of negro slaves increased and the

country developed. We who lived in the more
favored sections of these two states, under the
very shadows of the mountain peaks, know the
fallacy of these theories. It is true that the rigid
caste system which slavery always engenders between the slave-holder and the non-slave-holder
had its effect in driving back into the mountains
many who, through poverty or for conscience'
sake, belonged to the latter class; but Kentucky
was never a large slave-holding state, and to the
present day her foreign-born population and the
number of her citizens whose parents were foreign born is significantly small. These people
have the same ancestry and the same inheritance
as we. Surrounded by the same conditions of
life, they would be the same people. Or let me
reverse the picture. Take from *us*, or from *you*,
in whatever section of the country you may live,
the churches, the schoolhouses, and the good
roads which make contact with your neighbors
and the outside commercial world possible, for
one hundred years, and think, if you can, what
the result would be. Three generations of poverty, isolation, and neglect have left them where we
find them to-day—dwarfed physically, mentally,
and morally; their homes the same rude one or two
roomed log cabins, lighted by the open door, that
the early settlers found sufficient for their meager
and temporary wants; large families of men and
women, girls and boys, living in a single room.

In summer the little garden patch, which the women have made, some bacon, and occasionally a little fish or game, ' if the men about the place are not too shiftless ' and the river is ' nigh,' make a full larder. In winter generally bacon, some lard, sodden corn bread, varied by a nondescript thing which they call biscuit, made from the heavy, black flour that has been ground in the old water-mills, some coffee sweetened with honey, sorghum, or ' no sweet'nin',' the ever-present ' chaw ' of tobacco, and that scourge of the mountain, ' moonshine whisky,' supply the cravings of the inner man. What shall I say of the household furniture? Perhaps it were better left unsaid, as it rarely consists of more than a bench, a rickety table, a chair or stool, and some beds.

" In calling your attention to these facts I would not have you understand that all, or even a large majority, of the people in these mountains have suffered such degeneration or live as I have described. Far from it. Possibly one-half of what are called the mountain counties on both the Virginia and Kentucky sides of the Cumberland range have made a wonderful advance movement in the last fifteen or twenty years. Good roads, churches, and schoolhouses have been built, villages and towns have sprung up, or increased their population and business until even the ' back counties ' are beginning to be aroused from their lethargy, and to feel the tremor of an impending

change. Always, even in the darkest and most
inaccessible parts of this large section of country,
in the county-seats, and scattered here and there
throughout the counties, there have been some
men and women of strong intellect and character.
They have made comfortable homes, good estates,
sent their children away to school, and held an
acknowledged leadership in politics and business;
also in the barbarous feuds that have terrorized
whole regions of country.

" The Methodist circuit-rider has had his appointments among this people for three-quarters of
a century, working under untold difficulties, but
sowing the seed—some on stony ground, some
among thorns, and some, thank God! in good
ground—but the ' rocky ground ' has been the
largest part of this harvest-field. The stubble of
revival fires is always burning, but the great mass
of the people still remain unchanged. Along the
heads of the rivers, in the coves and narrow val-
leys, one-half the people can not read. The Holy
Scriptures are as an unknown tongue. The Prim-
itive, or ' Hard-Shell,' Baptist is the ruling denomination, and in one county their leaders preached
for seventy years without a ' church-house.'

" Within the last ten or fifteen years the public
school system is beginning to make itself felt in
these mountain wilds, and the members of the
Parsonage and Home Mission Society who have
been appointed to investigate, or who by reason of

lifelong proximity are familiar with the conditions
and needs of this section of country, believe that a
wise and Christian use of this great governmental
force is the best and surest channel through which
to civilize and redeem this neglected people. Each
of the different states through which this mountain
chain extends annually spends from one to two
millions of dollars on its public schools. By re-
cent enactments some of them have made it possible for the school commissioners to put a special
tax on each district to build and furnish the schoolhouse. These mountain people, even in the darkest localities, are by no means oblivious to the potent influence of money, and the brightest boys
and girls, the most influential families, want to secure the salary paid to the district school teacher.
In the thirty-two mountain counties of Kentucky
alone there are two hundred district schools. In
very many districts of the interior counties the local surroundings are such that only the native-born
teacher can fill the place. Of course they are to-
tally unqualified, and the rude people whose children they are supposed to teach recognize that a
fraud is being perpetrated on them. A sufficient
awakening to this condition of things has taken
place to make a change possible, and to prove a
golden opportunity to the Church if she will but
seize it. The mountains are demanding better
schools; the teachers, many of them, earnestly desire to be better qualified to hold their positions.

"The states do not furnish training-schools for these teachers, and if they did, in some of the large towns or cities the poverty, want of proper clothing, and fierce pride engendered by lifelong seclusion, would prove an insuperable barrier to these mountain folk. To evangelize and educate them, Christian people must establish high-grade schools in some of the principal towns or county-seats, adding, where possible, a few industrial features, and seeing to it that the teachers are well-equipped, progressive teachers, and earnest Christian men and women, who can put their spir-it, the Spirit of Christ, into these young teachers, who, going back to their respective homes, can have through the district schools opportunity to come into personal contact with every child and every household in the mountains. Let the houses in which these high-grade schools are taught—their furnishings, their surroundings—be object-lessons to the students, arousing in them the desire for better things, and creating a dissatisfaction with the old home life.

"Believing this to be the most effective way in which we can work, as a mission board, our soci-ety has established a school of this kind in Lon-don, Ky., the people of the town and the women of the Kentucky Conference furnishing the money for grounds and buildings, the same to be given in fee simple to the society, which is to maintain and control the school. Other points in this mountain

THE SUE BENNETT MEMORIAL SCHOOL, LONDON, KY.

range are pleading for the privilege of obtaining schools on the same terms, and urging that they will be entirely self-supporting in a few years. Our Church needs nothing so much as a united advance along all educational lines. These schools ought to be established, and with the cooperation of the Board of Education, correlated with such Conference institutions as it may direct. With a membership of 1,300,000, 900,000 of whom are women and girls, the Southern Methodist Church ought to do this work, and do it *now*. Our society is young and its collections small. Money we must have: and if the Church could be aroused to its opportunity and to its duty, this would be poured into our treasury until we would not have room enough to contain it."

Another important educational feature of this society is our work for the Cubans, who have come by the thousands from the island of Cuba to make their homes in an atmosphere free from oppression. At the second annual convention of the Woman's Parsonage and Home Missionary Society, which met at Nashville in October, 1894, Dr. Walter Lambuth gave, by request, an account of the conditions and needs of Cuba, and spoke of our mission as a Church to these neglected people. The soil had been prepared for this Cuban work several years previous by Dr. Palmore, Bishop Fitzgerald, and others, and so great was the interest awakened at the time of this convention that the ladies decided, in behalf of the Parsonage and Home Missionary Society, to undertake mission work among them at once. One thousand dollars was proposed to be raised by the pledging of one hundred $10 shares. Within fifteen minutes more than thirty shares were promised, and the remainder was raised later on for the establishment of two Cuban schools at Tampa, Fla. The superintendency of the work was then entrusted to Mrs. M. A. Wolff, of St. Louis, a wealthy and consecrated woman, whose daily prayers for years had been for the salvation of these oppressed people.

In a small way, the work was begun the very next month, and a mission school opened at Ybor City, Tampa. Mrs. Wolff rented a building, and, by personal outlay of $200, fitted it for occupancy, and two teachers who spoke Spanish were employed.

The second mission school was opened at Cuba City, a suburb of Tampa, in December, 1894, in the home of two Spanish women from Key West, Mrs. Rosa and Miss Emelina Valdes. They are earnest Christians, members of the Methodist Episcopal Church, South, and have taken the entire supervision of the school from the beginning.

One hundred and fifty children of Spanish descent were enrolled in the two schools the first year, and a gracious work accomplished.

The American Bible Society donated $25 worth

of Spanish and English Bibles, and the children were taught to read, and many of them to do excellent needlework, and other industries.

The second year of the work the corner-stone of a new and commodious building was laid at Ybor City. This building, valued at $7,000, is known as the Wolff Boarding-School. It is now well equipped in every department, kindergarten and industrial work being carried on, besides the teaching of the English branches of learning.

Cuban parents who send to these mission schools realize their extraordinary advantages, and, as a rule, the children manifest much interest in their studies and make rapid progress.

Mrs. Wolff has traveled extensively through Florida, organizing Parsonage and Home Mission Societies and Epworth Leagues, and endeavoring to enlist the young people of Florida in work for the conversion of the Cubans. She has also had the supervision of the two schools until, in April, 1897, on account of protracted illness, she asked to be relieved of her duties for a time, and Miss Mary W. Bruce, formerly missionary to Brazil, was put in charge of the Cuban Mission schools.

There are eighty-nine names enrolled in the elementary and grammar departments of the Wolff Mission School, and thirty-five in the kindergarten department. The same pupils attend Sunday-school at the mission church in that place. There are one hundred pupils enrolled at the school in

Cuba City, with an average attendance of seventy. The devotional exercises are conducted by the oldest pupils, who are showing great interest in the study of the Scriptures. There are Juvenile and Adult Parsonage and Home Mission Societies, and the Cubans are being taught to go out and do home mission work.

Mr. and Mrs. Valdes have donated a valuable lot for the building of a new chapel and school-room at West Tampa, which they have deeded to the Woman's Parsonage and Home Mission Society.

The greatest need in our Cuban work to-day is better accommodations for the boys. Miss Bruce is making appeals for this; and if the Church will respond, a grand work may be accomplished.

There are one hundred and twenty cigar-factories in West Tampa and Ybor City alone, and many young boys are at work in these.

What an opportunity this need affords for some able man or woman or society to assume the support of a Cuban school for boys! In the words of Rev. George B. Winton, missionary to Mexico, "the present need of the Cubans is the Church's opportunity." The impression which a little sympathy and help will make now on the hearts of these exiles can hardly be overestimated. Every child educated or fed or clothed will become, in a sense, a missionary. Every family administered to will give us a center of future operations, and the doors of their homes will ever swing open to the preaching of the gospel. It is a time for substantial, material help—the help of practical Christianity. The American missionary will be to the Cubans the representative of a people whom they already love, for the great heart of a people struggling for freedom has felt the answering heart-throb of another great nation rejoicing in freedom.

For twenty-five years we have been in Mexico, training men, translating books, printing tracts and periodicals, and acquiring experience. All this is now available. We tried to enter Venezuela, but the time was not ripe. It was too far away, and supervision too costly. Now Cuba is ready to be the bridge to Venezuela, to Central America, and all Spanish America—and if any part of America is our heritage as a Church, it is Spanish America. If it is possible for a Church to be effectually called, then this is our calling.

The latest educational enterprise of the Woman's Parsonage and Home Mission Society is the establishment of schools in California for the Chinese and Japanese. This work was begun in 1896, chiefly through the solicitations of our enterprising General Secretary, Mrs. R. K. Hargrove. In making a tour that year, and also in 1897, through the West with Bishop Hargrove as he had charge of the Western Conferences they had opportunities to study the field. Two night-schools were opened at Salinas and Oakland. Since, another has been

opened at Stockton, and work is being planned for a
school at Sacramento and other points. The Central
Committee has determined to labor for these foreigners through night-schools and Sunday-schools, and
group these together to be known as the Chinese
and Japanese Department of the Parsonage and
Home Mission Society. Rev. H. M. McKnight,
the superintendent of the work, writes: " Nothing in Salinas so interested the District Conference in 1896 as our mission school there. Our
Chinese attended all the sessions as interested
spectators. They sang and never let a collection
pass unheeded. They held a street meeting in
Chinatown, read the Scriptures in concert, prayed
in their native tongue, sang in choruses," etc. A
great work is before this society in the redemption of these foreigners for Christ.

Besides the educational department of this
great organization, very successful work has been
done in the way of city evangelization. In Dallas,
Tex., an institution is supported which has been
doing a noble work for fallen women. Funds
are now being raised to complete a large building.
The Treasurer writes: " This structure is magnificent in architectural design and proportion, and
ere long we shall have a house of mercy for the
oppressed and erring of which our Church and
even the state of Texas may be proud. The construction and maintenance of it has been under-
taken jointly by the North Texas, Northwest

THE MISSION HOME AT DALLAS, TEX.

9

Texas, and East Texas Conferences of the Woman's Parsonage and Home Mission Society." Only last year sixty girls were rescued there, thirty-two of whom were converted. They have in connection with the Rescue Home an industrial school and kindergarten for street waifs. Another large Rescue Home, under the auspices of this society, is located at San Antonio, Tex., and is doing a good work. A Door of Hope was established four years ago at Nashville, Tenn., through the efforts of two city missionaries employed by the society, Misses Emma and Tina Tucker. Other city missionaries are employed at Nashville, Tenn.; Macon, Ga.; New Orleans, La.; St. Louis, Mo.; and other places. These missionaries give their entire time to visiting jails, hospitals, and other charitable institutions, conducting Bible-readings, and, wherever practicable, establishing industrial and kindergarten schools.

Besides these various departments of home missionary work in successful operation at this date, the society has not neglected the work of building and assisting parsonages. During the year 1897 the amount loaned and donated by the Central Committee and the individual Conferences together was $16,621.81. In a letter received from the late Dr. David Morton, February 24, 1898, he says: "The showing of your work for the Church, in the matter of assisting parsonages, is certainly fine."

During the last quadrennium twice as many have been aided as during the previous eight years, and since the beginning of this woman's organization assistance has been rendered to this department to the amount of between $30,000 and $40,000.

The outlook for this society is great. But if we would realize in the future our highest aim and become, as our President says, " a vital force in the redemption of the world," we must arouse and gain the cooperation of that great body of women who call themselves Methodists and have taken the vows of the Church at her altars. If every one of the nine hundred thousand women of Southern Methodism were an intelligent and active member of this organization, not only America but the uttermost parts of the earth would see a great light in darkness, and we might look for the speedy coming of " new heavens and a new earth, wherein dwelleth righteousness."

At the annual convention of the society which met at Little Rock, Ark., in 1896, many testimonials of love and appreciation were given to the beloved founder of the Woman's Parsonage and Home Mission Society. A beautiful address was made in presenting the matter of raising a Named Loan Lund in her honor by the payment of $1,000. Pledges were immediately given in response to the amount of over $700. Throughout the Church, East, South, and West, the strongest and best

women and men in it had learned to know and
love her, and it filled her heart with gratitude and
sweet humility.

Thousands now echoed the sentiment of Dr.
David Morton's tribute to her: "When American
Methodism begins to scan the records and monu-
ments of the present century as curiously as we
are now scanning those of the century of Barbara
Heck and Madame Russell, not less conspicuous
among the names of the elect women who have
not only wrought well themselves but have exhibited the rarer grace of leadership, marshaling
armies of consecrated women to peaceful victory,
will be that of the indefatigable Kentucky woman
whose name is now loved and honored throughout
the entire Church."

CHAPTER VII.

*"How shall I do to love.' Believe. How shall I do to believe?
Love."—Leighton.*

SOME of the ripest work of Miss Helm's fertile brain was done through the paper she
edited during the last six years of her life. She
undertook the publishing of this paper in January,
1892, soon after the formation of the Woman's
Parsonage and Home Mission Society, and this
was one feature of the enterprise that elicited
much criticism. There was no money in the
treasury for it, and many insisted that the organization was not large enough to sustain a paper.
She felt confident, however, that it would add to
the interest and extension of the work, and at a
meeting of the Central Committee in September,
1891, the decision was made and she took measures to arrange for its publication.

She came to Nashville and spent a number of
days with Mrs. Harriet C. Hargrove and myself
while she made arrangements at the Methodist
Publishing House, and formulated her plans for
the first issue of the paper. I remarked to her
one day, as we were talking the matter over, that
I did not like the title she proposed giving the paper, *Our Homes*, and suggested in its stead " Our

Home Missions" or "Home Missions." She replied: "No, it is the homes of our country I have
been working for from the beginning; first it was
homes for our preachers, and now not only for
them but for the homeless, friendless, Christless,
thousands everywhere, and I want even the title of
my little messenger to bring that thought, the
thought of *home* to the front." She decided to
make her paper an eight-page quarterly, the subscription price to be twenty-five cents yearly.
Upon her return to Louisville she prepared the
first issue at the home of Mrs. George P. Kendrick, that friend rendering her practical assistance although the contributions and selections
were made entirely by herself. Three years later,
in order to be near the Publishing House, she
made Nashville her permanent home. In her in-
troductory paper she says with her characteristic
humility and sweetness of spirit: "Not as the as-
trologers of old seeking prophetic signs in the sky
among the stars, but striving as the Master said,
to 'discern the signs of the times,' we come into
the world of papers only to do the duty circumstances have made apparent. Ours is the first
paper, so far as we know, printed by our Church
in the interest of what we term "home missions," true home missions, we beg it to be understood, that do not hinder but rather build a
stronger foundation under foreign missions, by
removing that rock of offense to heathen lands:

a disbelieving, unjust nation back of the missionaries sent to them. We would in our humble way encourage a deeper, tenderer love for sinners by stressing personal effort in the salvation
of souls. We hope also, by serving as a means of
intercommunication, to unite the work our women
are doing at home; to systematize, concentrate,
and develop it. The method and system of our
efforts will be plain to those who will read our columns. Trusting we may ever show the spirit of
the Master, we ask to be received in his name.''

In this first issue she gives an article on '' Personal Christian Work,'' quoting as an introduc-
tion the following scripture: '' He first findeth his
own brother Simon, and saith unto him, We have
found the Messias, which is, being interpreted,
the Christ. And he brought him to Jesus.''
Thus in her first paper she gave the keynote according to her gamut of truth, for successful mission work, and she kept to the original theme
when her pen made its last stroke.

Her financial management of the paper was such
that within six months of the time it was determined
upon to have a paper it was put upon a paying basis. This very unusual occurrence proved but
another illustration of her practical wisdom and
economy. She never allowed herself or her work
to accumulate debts, and her record is clear from
beginning to end—a record of faith, love, the surmounting of difficulties, and final success.

She so arranged her paper as to accomplish a threefold mission: First, to represent the various departments of work carried on by the Woman's Parsonage and Home Mission Society as they progressed from month to month, including reports from the different Conferences relating to their individual work; secondly, she culled from other papers and books of a high grade material along the line of *home mission* work which proved interesting and stimulating; thirdly, she gave her own editorial articles, which showed her to be abreast with the times, and far-sighted in her views of the problems of our country and how to meet them. From the first issue of her paper she alloted a space to the children. It is a matter of remark that during all her busy life she was ever mindful of children and invalids, and sought their cooperation in her work. The same spirit that showed itself away back in her childhood in the care of insignificant things that were neglected by others, made her a friend to the helpless in her ripe womanhood. She frequently wrote the beautiful little stories for the children's department of her paper. In recognition of help given by children she never failed to give their reports. In speaking of assistance rendered by invalids she says in the April number of 1894: "When our Parsonage and Home Mission Society began its work, those who first came to its aid were our dear shut-in ones, and with the contributions sent by them we were able to give shelter to a number of our homeless brethren." In the Christmas number (1892) of her paper (the fourth issue) she gives an exquisite scrap of solace to *homeless hearts*. She says:

" It may be that this little Christmas sheet will come under the eye of one in whose life even at this time when all make merry there comes no gladness. A heavy burden lies upon your soul this day, while memory's tears fill your eyes, and thoughts of the home of your childhood stir your heart and its 'ever-restless beating is a sad, sad prayer for peace.' This day peace shall come to you, even you, for

Restless hearts, God is Peace.

Weary hearts, weary hearts, by the cares of life oppressed, this day you may find sweetest rest, for this day in the long ago came One who spoke as never man spake: ' Come unto me, all ye that are weary and heavy-laden, and I will give you rest.'

Weary hearts, God is Rest.

And you broken hearts, so desolate and lone, sitting in the home whence joy is fled, bowed down by sorrow, listening to low voices from the past that o'er your present ruins moan, to you this day speaks the Christ who came to bind up the brokenhearted. Lift up your eyes. Heaven is around you, for he is with you.

Broken hearts, God is Joy.

No home where loved ones gather! No home

where fond memories cluster! A stranger at the
banquet board, an alien at the fireside, a wanderer
upon the street; God help you, homeless one,
wherever you may be this day!

Homeless hearts, homeless hearts, through the dreary, dreary
  years,
Ye are lonely, lonely wand'rers, and your way is wet with
  tears.
In bright and gladsome places, wheresoever ye may roam,
Ye look away from earth-land, and ye murmur: 'Where is
  home;'
          Homeless hearts, God is Home."

In 1893 her paper was issued monthly, beginning with the August number. The subscription-
price was increased to fifty cents. There is a
very marked advance shown through the paper
this year in every line of work carried on by the
society. Words of kind appreciation were sent
daily to the editor for the good developed in different places through its agency. Women who had
hitherto been content with their daily round of duties, and had never thought it possible for them to
branch out beyond these, were so inspired by reading in its columns what others were doing, that
the narrow circles of their own lives became widened, and they enthusiastically engaged in branches of work represented by this connectional enterprise. Miss Helm solicited the interest of the
" King's Daughters'" societies (to which she belonged, always wearing the little silver cross), the
Epworth Leagues, and other societies, and began

to realize that this loved work of *home missions*
in our Church was being recognized by many
Christian organizations in the country. Exchange
was made with a number of Northern and Eastern
missionary publications, until *Our Homes* had at
least a bowing acquaintance with many prominent
workers in the great fields of Christian activity.
Her bright spirit, even when she was attacked by
criticism, and her quick, good-humored repartee
were always refreshing. In an article published
this year of 1893 in the *Richmond Advocate* the
editor says: "Miss Helm, in making appeals
through her paper for parsonages, now and then
sends us harrowing accounts of women and children, the wives and offspring of Methodist preachers, living in sheds and bitten by hungry winter
weather on the frontier. In Oklahoma, she says,
'Rev. Mr. Brewer leaves his wife in poor health in
a tent, and he goes up and down that wild country preaching.' She adds: 'In that bleak climate
a delicate woman is in fearful condition without
roof or shelter.' No doubt of it. The next
specimen is a wife and babes in an old abandoned
house, little better than a shed, impossible to make
comfortable in winter. Well, these tales are harrowing. Miss Helm's feelings were no doubt
harrowed before she sent them, but the first instance was given as a direct quotation from a letter written by Dr. John, Secretary of the Board
of Missions; the second taken from a letter sent

her by Mrs. Bishop Haygood, and I do not doubt
the statements; but my idea as to how the trouble
may be prevented is this: There are two or three
sides to this question. In the name of humanity,
why do men with a spark of mercy drag a delicate woman and babes to such horrors? No man
is called of God to be a brute. Go alone. Leave
a wife under some roof in a Christian community.
If a man intends to do this mission work, why
does he hinder his work, disgrace himself, scan-
dalize the decencies of life, by persuading a good
woman to marry him, and then haul the poor
thing and her little ones among barbarians, with
less comforts than a farm cow? When Asbury
led his band of pioneers in blazing a path for
Methodism in civilized Virginia and the Caroli-
nas, only three out of eighty were married men.
Marriage is a luxury. The advice of 'old Paul,'
as the sweet spinsters who prance on platforms
sneeringly call him, seems a back number to the
modern missionary. The Church needs single
men. The good cause wanes because Methodism
can not find a band of brave old bachelors as in
the heroic age of the Church. There are evils in
the celibacy of the Romish priesthood, yet men
give credit for this self-denial. Its origin had
high motive. There is leak and loss at this point
in our Church.''

Miss Helm responds to the article as follows:
'' The Doctor is right. That is certainly the alter-

native, if our parsonage-building movement is not
by our ministers encouraged and kept up. The
Methodist Church, if we understand the matter,
is not quite ready to accept the Romish priesthood. Yet the Church can not step out of the
forward march of Christianity. It must send the
gospel, must carry forward the banner of Christ;
and that ' band of brave old bachelors,' like many
another good thing, appears to be altogether ideal
and not ready for the present practical emergencies. What then? Our Parsonage and Home
Mission Society must come to the rescue. Its
existence becomes an absolute necessity, for if
men and their families must and will go into these
places to carry the gospel to dying souls at any
cost, we must help them. It is heroic to suffer
yourself, but cruel to leave others to suffer, and
the Doctor does not wish these wives and little
ones to suffer. We will not mind about the im-
proper individuals who ' prance,' but at the same
time appear to be carrying out the Doctor's idea of
Pauline practise, because if they were so irrever-
ent as to call one of the inspired writers ' old Paul'
they deserve to have the Doctor quote them, and
that is all he does."

The June number of this year is an extra—published to give the proceedings of the first convention, that met in St. Louis. It gives in full several
addresses made, and is inspiring in its account of
the phenomenal success of the work.

In the August number she says: "With this
number *Our Homes* begins its monthly series.
Eighteen months ago it began its existence with
fear and trembling. It had faith enough, but was
not sure of its 'call.' Before the close of the year
friendly greetings from all quarters had given it
much assurance. This year began propitiously.
'Let us have a monthly' was the demand from
every direction. Feeling that it can in no future
emergency be accused of rashness by the most
cautious, strengthened by the honest conviction
that its call was of God and that he will through
its pages work good to many souls, it will try
humbly and faithfully to be but an instrument in
his hands for doing good."

Words of earnest commendation like the following from the *Methodist Review of Missions* were
frequently sent to the now successful paper:
"The St. Louis Convention, held in May, was so
important that we give space to Miss Helm's report. 'The Church a Missionary Society, and
Every Church-Member a Missionary' is their
motto. Who dare be so small as to make invid-
ious comparisons in favor of or against home or
foreign missions? 'The Son of man came to
seek and to save that which is lost.' A man may
be as much lost in New Orleans as in Calcutta, or
in the Pan Handle of Texas as on the steppes of
Tartary. Away with the narrow-minded bigotry
that looks askance at one who attempts to reach

down and touch poor submerged women in the
slums of our cities and canonizes the missionary
who has lived and worked, perchance, in beautiful Japan or sunny Mexico. Go on, brave wom-
en, until you have beleagured and taken every
Southern city for Christ and converted every parsonage and home into a Christian stronghold.''

Her editorials toward the close of this second
year are worthy of especial notice. In one of
them she says:

''Our Lord said, as he left this world, 'As
my Father hath sent me, even so I send you;'
'Preach the gospel to every creature.' Do not
let us be alarmed at the word 'preach.' Would
that so much precious time were not lost discuss-
ing words and privileges! Preaching does not
necessarily imply a large audience or a public
stand. Christ preached one of his most spiritual
sermons to one woman—one sinful woman. Every Christian man, woman, or child is not only
free to preach the gospel, but under command to
see that this gospel is given to every creature within his reach. The knowledge of the way of salvation is the key to the kingdom of heaven. It is
in your hand. If you refuse to use it to open the
kingdom to any soul as far as lies in your power,
you have condemned that soul to death.

''There is in this prosperous land of ours no town
so small that you may not find many needing your
ministration, and there is no city within our bounds

so well supplied with earnest Christian workers
but that there is need for more, need for *you*. It
is appalling to think how many thousands are going down to eternal death within easy walk of our
doors, while we—God help us! What are we
doing? Enjoying ourselves! Dancing on the
graves of the dead, making shrouds into ball-
dresses! Serving self as if we did not remember
there was anything like sin and death in this gay,
busy world of ours. Yes, ours, we think it is, to
do with it as we choose. Perhaps it is persecution we need to purify the Church and arouse us
to a remembrance of the value of the truth that
has been committed to our care, or a little review
of the history of the early Christians who were
called upon to give their lives for the gospel's
sake, who risked all their possessions to worship
Christ, and preferred death to bowing to the false
gods of this world, standing unmoved before the
gaudy pageantry of its power. It is true that some
are not idlers in Zion, some of us have tried faithfully to do our duty; but there were grievous obstacles to be overcome, and it is sometimes difficult to know which way duty lies. Let us take
counsel together as to how best to succeed in doing this work for our Father and encourage each
other to persevere, knowing that the truth as it is
in Christ shall triumph at last. And let us keep
his words in mind, as we know he was sent to
suffer, sent to bind up the broken-hearted, sent to

10

preach the gospel to the poor, sent to seek and to save the lost. '*As my Father hath sent me, even so send I you.*' "

In this second year's paper she gives an account of the Scarritt Bible and Training School and much of the work done by the Misses Tucker and others employed by our society in city evangelization. She makes frequent and strong appeals for this work to be carried on more vigorously by the society, and gives in the February number of 1894, and also in the June number, selections from the diary of the Misses Tucker in behalf of this work. No outcasts of society could become so degraded as not to elicit her pity and her help, inasmuch as the Master had reached out his hand to save them. In the June issue she gives a selection called " Homes for the Fallen," from which we copy the following extract: "On Thursday night, February 5, a young woman not more than thirty years old tottered into a wretched restaurant. She was dreadfully emaciated, but her delicate features indicated that she had been well born. She was poorly clad, but her clothes were clean. She dragged herself into the cheap restaurant and said to the keeper: 'John, I am cold and hungry; I want a cup of coffee, but I have not a cent.' 'All right, you shall have it,' he said. She sunk into a seat and as the coffee was brought drew from her pocket a dried crust of bread and tried to bite it. She had not strength.

She dipped it in the coffee and took a bite, then put the rest in her pocket, after which she stretched forth her hand for the coffee; but it fell, and with a little scream she died. In her pocket were some Salvation Army leaflets and a card from the Salvation Army on which was written:

> 'All have sinned—
> Look! Unto me,
> Live! Jesus saves.'

This was all, except a piece of paper on which were the following lines:

> ' On the street, on the street;
> To and fro with weary feet;
> Aching heart and aching head;
> Homeless, lacking daily bread;
> Lost to friends and joy and name;
> Sold to sorrow, sin, and shame;
> Wet with rain and chilled by storm;
> Ruined, wretched, lone, forlorn;
> Weak and wan with weary feet,
> Still I wander on the street,
>
> On the street, on the street,
> Whither tend my wand'ring feet.
> Love and hope and joy are dead,
> Not a place to lay my head;
> Every door against me sealed.
> Hospital and Potter's field—
> These stand open. Wider yet
> Swings perdition's yawning gate;
> Thither tend my wandering feet.
> On the street, on the street!
>
> On the street, on the street,
> Might I here a Saviour meet?

From the blessed far-off years
Comes the story of her tears
Whose sad heart with sorrow broke,
Heard the words of love he spoke,
Heard him bid her anguish cease,
Heard him whisper, "Go in peace."
O that I might kiss his feet,
On the street, on the street!'

The fathomless agony voiced in these lines gives
us a hint of what this poor girl suffered, and
yet we know her suffering is the suffering of tens
of thousands, while many of us go along without
the faintest idea of human brotherhood and sister-
hood when appeals are made to save the sinking
masses."

During this year of 1894 she received for the
paper a number of strong articles from several of
the bishops and other influential men of the
Church in behalf of the great work carried on by
the society. In one of these, by Bishop Granbery, he says, in speaking of the week of prayer
appointed by the society: "Give ear, preachers
and people! A claimant presents herself to whom
you have given too little time and money. She is
the Parsonage and Home Mission Society. Have
you accorded her recognition? Her petition just
now is that one week, the Week of Prayer, may
be set apart in all your pastoral charges for the
benefit of the noble cause she serves. This week
is to be employed in daily religious meetings, special prayer, and cheerful donations. This society

is endeavoring to provide a home for every married itinerant sent forth to preach the word. Our women are doing good in behalf of foreign missions, but love of the heathen abroad should never be a plea for neglect of neighbors and countrymen. Preachers in charge, is there a Parsonage and Home Mission Society in your station or circuit? The Week of Prayer will furnish an excellent opportunity to increase its membership. If there be none, it will be a good time to supply the lack."

One paragraph from Bishop Wilson's appeal reads: "The Woman's Parsonage and Home Mission Society begs a larger hearing from the Church. By every token it is entitled to it. Governed by no selfish motive, looking to no mere local interest, it proposes to contribute along its own line of endeavor (and that may mean of sacrifice) to the furtherance of the one great work of the gospel to which the entire Church is committed. Men and brethren, ye that fear God and love our Lord Jesus Christ, help these women who labor with us in the gospel." The paper kept before its readers in 1894 the *Reading Course*, which had just been instituted, gave the history and development of the various *loan funds*, the reports and addresses of the second annual convention that met in Nashville, the new work inaugurated during that convention, and other matters of interest.

In the next year's paper the reports from the various Conferences and extracts from letters to

the General Secretary show an increase of work
along each line.   Frequent articles are given from
the pen of the gifted President, Mrs. E. E. Wiley,
who created much interest through her pen as
well as through her earnest addresses in behalf of
the work.

In the May number Miss Belle H. Bennett
writes strongly on "Our Opportunities in the
Mountains of Kentucky." Miss Helm says, in
making an appeal for that work in a later issue:
"The offer of the people of London, Ky., to
raise $20,000 for site and building for a high-
grade school, if the Parsonage and Home Mission
Society will raise an endowment fund of $20,000,
was presented before the Central Committee by
Miss Belle Bennett, the ardent friend of our mountain regions.   She has studied the situation and
become more and more impressed with the obligations resting upon Christians to aid these people
in surmounting the many natural obstacles to their
progress.   The small endowment of $20,000 should
be easily raised.   The expressed interest of friends
from every quarter point to early success in securing this endowment, which will make the school
self-supporting.   All who wish to remedy the neglect of years toward these needy ones in our midst
should rally at once and act without delay.   God
only can calculate the harvest of souls that may
be gathered through the agency of this school.
Pray for it, friends, everywhere, and work for it.

The need is imperative that we women of Southern Methodism should rally with a God-loving enthusiasm to the help of our poor young sisters cut off from the opportunities and prosperity of other regions of the South. Our superintendent of the mountain work, who is loved and admired by the whole Church, is throwing the full force of her strong character into this work for the mountain people, because she loves and sympathizes with them in their sore straits. She has made many untold sacrifices for them We must not close our eyes to this much-needed work. Our helpless sisters are reaching out their hands to us in mute appeal to be lifted out of their ignorance and poverty. How dare we turn our backs upon them? Will God forgive us if we do not help them now? Delay means that many more shall suffer and be lost while we wait—for what? God's hand is not shortened. It is our feeble, pulseless hands that are at fault. Reach them out to save. Lift them up to receive. Fill your hearts with love to God and man, that divine life may flow through every pulse-giving power from on high."

Surely such strong appeals as this, coming through the organ of the society, had much to do with the permanent establishment and success of that school, and will help to mature plans for raising the much-needed endowment.

Besides writing about every department of the work, she kept the hearts of her readers turned

toward the ever-living Source of success through
her editorials. Her earnest heart-cries for the
home might be heard as an undertone through all
her writings. She who found her own home in
doing the will of God had the profoundest sympathy for those who knew no happy shelter they
could call home. In one of her editorials in the
July number of 1895 she says:

"It should be the first mission of every woman
to win her home for Christ. It is well to undertake great things for God, but not well to overlook
the seeming little things that, done for Christ's
sake, may become greater than we could plan.
While the hearts of children are tender their in-
nocent eyes look up to their mother's and their
little hands cling to her, and then is the mother's
opportunity. Those precious souls then are hers.
Claim them for Christ, O Christian mothers, before the world draws them away from you or
the evil one plucks them out of your hand.
These lives are as potter's clay in your hands
then, and every touch of your fingers will show
when age has hardened them. A mother grew
angry with her baby boy for pressing the tip of his
tiny finger into the yet soft paint on the door.
The painter was gone. It could not be remedied.
The print of the little finger must remain, and the
print of her anger and injustice remained on his
soul. 'Go away,' she said as he clung to her,
crying, not knowing how to explain that he did not

know it was so very wrong, and he wanted her love. ' Go away,' she said then and many times afterward, when consumed with household cares or selfish entertainment. And he went away, and continued to go away from home until she would gladly have seen his soiled footprints upon the daintiest carpet in the house she had striven to keep spotless, while she had let the pure white soul become sullied with sin. Awakening too late to use the mother's love for which the baby had pleaded, she begs in quivering tones of her pastor: ' Oh, save my boy!'

" Will he come back, or will he go away forever? The mercy of God is great. The most hardened may be won back by prayer and faithful, watchful love. On you first, mother, wife, sister, depends the winning of your home for Christ. Be Christ's representative in your own home. Be the watchman in that home, ready to call for God's help at the least appearance or dread of evil. When our homes are Christ's, our country will easily be won for him."

Although Miss Helm kept the interests of the society ever before the Church through her paper, she did not devote the entire space to its work. Her sympathies were broad, and she gave her readers, as often as possible, articles and selections on the temperance movement, Salvation Army work, kindergarten methods, and other philanthropies of national interest. She also gave sketches

of the lives of prominent writers, and selections
from their works: Helen Hunt Jackson, Miss F. R.
Havergal, Madame Guyon, " Sister Dora," Rev.
F. B. Meyer, and others. Her book reviews were
especially good. She reviewed the books in our
Reading Course and other philanthropic works,
and also gave selections from Tolstoi's writings,
Ian Maclaren's, and others. An account of the
life and work of her intimate friend, Miss Jennie
Casseday, was given in one issue of the paper.
We copy the following beautiful extract relating to
the work of the Louisville Flower Mission, established by Miss Casseday: " The members of the
Louisville Flower Mission while making their charitable visits see and hear many pathetic things.
One day a lady went to the western portion of the
city to take a basket of groceries and fruit to a sick
woman. Making a mistake in the address, she
found on getting off the car that she was not in the
right place, so she stopped at a house to make in-
quiries. She was told that, although the person
she was seeking did not live in the neighborhood,
there was a family on the opposite side of the street
that was certainly suffering. Accordingly she
crossed over, and found standing at the gate a little
golden-haired fellow about four years old. He
was looking anxiously and expectantly down the
street. When he saw her his countenance bright-
ened, and, looking earnestly into her face, said
in an awe-struck tone, ' Did God send you?'

' Yes, God sent me,' was the reply. ' Have you brought the bread?' Receiving an answer in the affirmative, he rushed into the house crying joyfully : ' Mama, mama, God has sent the bread.' The lady followed him into a room where a poor woman lay sick and suffering. By her side was a baby only a few days old, and another of two years was sitting on the floor. They had no coal in the house, and nothing to eat. The father was out trying to find work. When the children had cried for something to eat, the poor mother had told them to be good and God would send them bread. The little fellow had been out at the gate watching ever since.''

In the August and October numbers of 1895 are given accounts of the *Cuban Mission* schools; the proceedings of the third annual convention of the society, at Asheville, N. C.; the address in full of H. B. Someillan, the converted Spaniard, and his grand work for his countrymen. In her account of her visit to the Cuban schools we have a fair view of their present prosperity and her gratitude for it. While in Florida she met Dr. Buckley, editor of the *New York Christian Advocate*, and gave him some account of our work for the Cubans. He was very much interested, and gave a favorable notice of it in the *Christian Advocate* on his return to New York. Miss Helm writes from Florida concerning the Wolff mission school: '' It was a treat for me to go into Miss Perrin's kinder-

garten room and see the large number of little ones
being led gently by kindergarten principles to a
knowledge of the truth by a woman so admirable
in Christian character. In a room where higher
branches are taught, a girl was at the blackboard
explaining the construction of an English sentence
with such ease and understanding that a lady who
accompanied us whispered: ' I could not have done
that myself.' These girls are also being taught the
power of sincere, frank, straightforward Christian
womanhood. The opening for good is incalcula-
ble.

" Does this work not repay us for the outlay of
funds, and should it not be a comfort to our beloved Mrs. Wolff, who, led of God, laid this mission on the hearts of the women of the Church
and has contributed so largely her time, strength,
and money for its success?"

The April number of this year is made up entirely of contributions by some of the leading men
of the Church: Bishops Key, Hargrove, Hendrix,
Fitzgerald, Granbery, Duncan, Dr. David Morton, Dr. Barbee, and others. It is also illustrated by their photographs, and closes with a selection from President Cleveland's address on "Home
Missions," given at the meeting of the Board of
Home Missions of the Presbyterian Church in
New York City. This is a unique number, and
many extra copies were sold. About this time there
were many papers and journals issuing "woman's

editions" to raise money for their various enterprises, and it was Miss Helm's happy thought to
vary the matter and get out a "*man's edition*" of
her paper. It gives a consensus of opinion by
some of the dignitaries of the Church concerning
the "Parsonage and Home Mission Society," its
history, its field, its successes, and its possibilities.
The *Wesleyan Christian Advocate*, in speaking
of this edition, says: "The special edition of
Our Homes, issued the 1st of April, is certainly a
beautiful and attractive paper. The editor, Miss
Helm, has made a success of every number, and
deserves the thanks and abundant patronage of
the Church for her noble work. In this special
issue, besides the range of articles, she has the
best pictures of our bishops we have seen."

The *St. Louis Christian Advocate* and a number of other papers gave frequent complimentary
notices of *Our Homes*. One Alabama paper says
of it: "*Our Homes* is doing good work as a lit-
erary power in our Church. The 'man's edition'
is a new venture in periodical literature, and is a
fine specimen of a paper, whether considered as
to its variety and range of articles, illustrations, or
its general appearance." In the December number of 1896 she gives an article on missions for
the Chinese in California, in which she says:
"As we read of the work done and yet to be done
for the Chinese, a burning desire fills our hearts
that our women too may enlarge their efforts for

these needy people. God has sent them to us to
receive of us the bread of life. Shall we say, ' Let
others give it,' or shall we be eager to serve at the
Lord's table?'' She then quotes from two leaflets on the Chinese in California, the last one
being the sad history of a Chinese slave girl, called
"A Sketch of Ah Yute." It brings out vividly
the horrors of the slave practise among these
young girls, and how this one was rescued by
home mission workers, and became a Christian
just before her death.

Miss Helm was greatly rejoiced when the society, in 1896, opened schools at Salinas and Oakland, in response to the energy and efforts of our
General Secretary, Mrs. R. K. Hargrove, and
every feature of the work in those schools was of
deep interest to her. She made appeals for the
Chinese mission work in her articles published in
Church papers before the Parsonage and Home
Mission Society was ever organized, and in the
last paper she ever sent to the press, December,
1897, she gives a selection from the Pacific mission about that work. There was no class nor condition of mankind, no race nor color, that did not
have the sympathy and consideration of this great-
hearted woman. In the September number of
the last year she writes a very suggestive article on
the "Negro Problem." We quote a few para-
graphs: " In missionary work in Northern cities
the foreign element gives problems hardest to

solve. We of the South find in our negro element
one of our hardest missionary problems. It has
been complicated by certain theories and senti-
ments inconsistent with facts. . . . But, re-
gardless of causes, of misunderstandings, or of
prejudices, we must remember that the worse their
condition, the more they need our help as Christians, the more incumbent upon us is the duty of
lifting them up. They need religious instruction.
That they are capable of reaching a higher standard of character is shown by their record in the
past, and by those who to-day are benefactors of
their race. The work of such men as Rev. Book-
er Washington should prompt us to help this race
more actively than we as women of the Church
have done. God help us to do it!''

In one of her editorials we have an example of
her ability to think in philosophic lines. It is entitled " Omega," and is as follows: " If a God
did not make this universe, believe me, this great
self-developing universe must ultimately make a
God. If, as the theory of evolution would lead us
to believe, some incomprehensible force in crude
atoms could produce man—man with the mental
power to comprehend the wonderful revelations of
science, man with the spiritual force to conceive
the idea of the God of Christianity, such a man
as Jesus of Nazareth—who shall say that this marvelous evolution shall stop there? Whose hand
has been reached out to stay its onward progress?

Whose voice shalt say: 'Thus far shalt thou go,
and no farther?' Shall not the self-propelling development go on until the innate force of man
shall evolve the good that his mind has conceived
as surely and as substantially as the mindless beginnings have evolved the real man as he is, sur-
veying, weighing, judging all things? The distance from man to God is not so great as from the
protoplasm to the mind of the scientist and the
philosopher. Thus the theory of evolution, even
as held by materialists, would bring mankind to
Christ Jesus and through him to the Omega and
he shall be able to say: 'In the beginning before
the world was, I am,' for he himself was in that
first movement of life that was to result in the all-
comprehending spirit mind. He shall be able to
say: 'I was in all. My love was through all. I
was the *force*, the Alpha that bore on the process
of development until it reached the Omega. In
me all things end. Around me all things circle.
With me all things began, and without me there
was not anything made that was made.' From God
there is no escape. Conceal him in ' force,' and
he reveals himself in results. Who can fail to
recognize the fact that, trusted to even a blind
force, man has attained to that high plane of development that stands midway between God and
man in Jesus of Nazareth, before whose sublime
character infidels bow as to the peerless among
men, and in the fulness of time God, uniting him-

self with man in the God-man, has opened the way for man to become a new creature."

The paper for 1897 gives her last work. There are many valuable contributions from her pen during this year, but we think we can discern a minor strain through all the halleluiahs. Her health was extremely delicate; and, although she made no complaint, she said to us more than once: "God is preparing my paper. I just have to lie down and ask him to arrange it."

The April or Easter number is especially attractive. One selection of poetry is entitled "What Christ Said to Me," and is as follows:

> I said, "Let me walk in the fields;"
> He said, "No, walk in the town."
> I said, "There are no flowers there;"
> He said, "No flowers, but a crown."
> I said, "But the skies are black,
> There is nothing but noise and din;"
> And he wept as he sent me back.
> "There is more," he said, "there is sin."
> I said, "But the air is thick,
> And the fogs are veiling the sun;"
> He answered, "Yet souls are sick,
> And souls in the dark undone."
> I said, "I shall miss the light,
> And friends will miss me, they say;"
> He answered, "Choose to-night
> If I am to miss you, or they."
> I pleaded for time to be given;
> He said, "Is it hard to decide?
> It will not seem hard in heaven
> To have followed the steps of your Guide."

She gives a sweet, pathetic picture of the mis-

11

sion of a flower under the caption "Cast Down:"
"It was an early spring day. There was still a
lingering touch of winter in the chill air. Through
thin clouds the sunlight came weak and pale.
The leaves underfoot had lost the crisp rustle of
autumn, and lay sodden and heavy on the earth.
The world looked gray and sad. On a decaying
log at the edge of the woods on the brink of the
hill sat a man. He was growing old. His life
had been full of sorrow. He had borne it bravely. He had burdened no one with his grief, but it
had sunk into his heart like the sodden leaves
upon the earth. He had come out of the dull
house to seek comfort in nature. He looked
slowly around upon the scene, but it gave him no
pleasure now. His head sunk upon his breast
and he sat in deep reverie. He remembered the
day when earth was bright and beautiful to him,
and his heart buoyant with the light of the Christian's love to God. The light had faded and the
joy gone. All was death within, without, above,
below. A mourner he sat by the grave of the
love that once bade him look up to God and smile.
He moved his feet slowly among the dead leaves.
They so aptly expressed to him his own life. With
a start of surprise he saw peeping out from under
the leaves a violet, fresh and blue. Could it be
that under the dead leaves of sorrow and discouragement in his own soul life and love were hidden
as the violet under the leaves that he need but

throw aside? He looked up as one awakening from sleep. The sun was shining warm and bright. There was a movement in the air as if the buds upon the trees were breathing new life. A bird overhead began to sing. He stooped and picked up the violet. With a grateful smile he looked over the beautiful earth, and at the sky so blue and bright. The tiny flower had brought its lesson of divine love, blooming above and beneath the sorrows and cares of life."

The October number of this last year is one of the most beautiful and instructive ever given her readers. In a very effective article entitled "If Ye Love Me" she gives as an advanced idea of Church work the one known as the "Institutional Church" and the description of its methods of work in the Grace Baptist Church of Philadelphia, known as "Conwell Temple." This church has developed a wider system of ministries than can be found anywhere else in America. When a person connects himself with it he is given a card of membership and receives a book containing a schedule of the different ways of working, on which he is invited to indicate the work he will undertake. The principle of this church is to minister as far as possible to every kind of human need. Miss Helm adds: "Our Southern Methodist Church is an institutional Church in one sense. It is well prepared, with its many institutions, to become a strong working force for Christ.

With its Parsonage and Home Mission Society
and Epworth League, if thoroughly vivified and util-
ized by stirring and spiritual pastors, it could do
much of the work of the new institutional Church.
Here too our Church Extension Board comes forward to aid in building up the Lord's kingdom; and
to carry the good news to the uttermost parts of the
earth, we have our vigorous Woman's Foreign
Missionary Society; and fostering all at home and
abroad, the General Board of Missions. As our
Church government is in no sense congregational,
it is equipped on the idea that the world is our par-
ish. But there needs to be through the whole a
pervading spirit uniting all departments in this
great work to make it move forward an irresistible
force for Christ."

She gives, in an article that follows this one, the
large scope of work possible and intended by the
Woman's Parsonage and Home Mission Society.

It may be truly said of Miss Helm that she went
to her desk as to an altar, and her prayer concerning her paper was: "Help me, O Father, to make
Our Homes a *voice* that shall be heard throughout
the Church in defense of the weak and helpless, and
of entreaty for the outcast and sinner." And surely her prayer was answered. We give as a last
selection from her editorial work one of her great,
heart-throbbing calls to keep close to God. "Come,
tired hearts," she says, "let us rest, and think of
our Father's home. You have labored all the

year for your Lord. You are weary in the contest with sin and sorrow. You are heartsore from
great sacrifices made for truth and righteousness—
sacrifices that went deep into your life. God only
knows how deep, but he does know. He knows
all the pain, the weariness, the tears, the sorrow.
You weep silently on your pillow when the darkness covers you as a veil; but he sees, he listens,
he speaks: ' Be still and know that I am God. I
have loved thee with an everlasting love, therefore
with loving-kindness have I drawn thee?' ' Is suffering the language of love?' you moan. Yes, it
was your Saviour's language. Shall you not speak
in the same language back to him? It must needs
be so, beloved. He who strives to reach heaven
through this world where sin reigns must stem a
current as strong as death, and break through a
net the meshes of which are closely interwoven
between one's own sin and the sin of others until
his very heart-strings break in the struggle to be
free and press heavenward, But Christ came to
pass on before us that we might see the way by
the light of his radiant love. He suffered that we
might know he understands all about our suffer-
ings. But for him suffering would have no meaning, sorrow no hope, truth and love no triumph.

"Perfect through suffering, our salvation's seal
Set in the front of His humanity;
But if, impatient, thou let slip thy cross,
Thou wilt not find it in this world again,

Nor in another. Here, and here alone,
Is given thee to *suffer* for God's sake.
Canst thou not suffer then one hour? or two?
If he should call thee from thy cross to-day,
Saying, " It is finished—that hard cross of thine
From which thou prayest for deliverance,"
Thinkest thou not some passion of regret
Would overcome thee? Thou wouldst say:
    " So soon?
Let me go back and suffer yet a while,
More patiently; I have not yet praised God."

" Let us then, beloved, learn our lesson well while
we are here. Press forward bravely, true heart.
The goal is worth all and more than you can be
called to endure, for remember he said: ' I go to
prepare a place for you.'

" O precious Saviour, a place for *me?* a place in
my Father's house prepared by thy loving hands?
How beautiful! how blessed to contemplate!

Jerusalem, the golden,
  I toil on night and day,
Heartsore each night with longing,
  I stretch my hands and pray
That midst thy leaves of healing
  My soul may find its rest
Where the wicked cease from troubling
  And the weary are at rest.

"And we are coming nearer to it, sisters, day by
day. We see its foundation of glittering gems.
Like a great inverted rainbow, all glorious to behold, formed by the light of God's smile on earth's
sorrow clouds, it encircles Zion, city of our God.
Beyond the gates of pearl we catch entrancing

glimpses of the white forms of those who have
gone before us. They stand by the great white
throne. Under the leaves of healing they walk by
the river of life clear as crystal. As a whisper of
peace to our souls we hear the voice of the Infinite say: 'God shall wipe away all tears from
their eyes; and there shall be no more death, neither sorrow, nor crying, neither shall there be any
more pain: for the former things are passed
away.' ''

CHAPTER VIII.

TWILIGHT.

"The weary sun hath made a golden set."—Shakespeare.

ERE the lengthening shadows of evening gather about this noble life, let us take our last view of Lucinda Helm as a *woman*, separate and apart from her identification with Christian work; and catch, if we can, the charm of that personality that so vivified everything she touched, and not only won for her hosts of friends, but united them to her in an indissoluble bond. In the first place, we observe the superior gifts and graces illustrated in her personal friendships. She was *true* to her friends, whether in their presence or absence, seeking their welfare at all times before her own. Faithfulness was woven into the very texture of her being. She lived in an atmosphere too high for duplicity or selfish interests of any sort, and no absorption in the great cause for which she labored made her forget or neglect the obligations of personal friendships. Her honesty and transparency of nature as exhibited in this relationship made her peculiarly lovable. We leaned upon her. We weighted her unintentionally but instinctively with responsibilities. We carried to her our burdens, feeling sure always of her direct communication with the great Burden-Bearer. Her loving sympathy at all times, her profound adherence to the right, her gentleness and her unwavering faith made her friendship invaluable. No wonder that all our Gordian knots were given into her patient and skilful hands. When she was called home scores of women throughout the entire Church sustained a *personal* loss.

One of the most beautiful characteristics of her nature was cheerfulness. Although frail and delicate throughout life, her spirit so completely dominated her body that she never complained or was gloomy, and rarely alluded to her ill health. She possessed an elasticity, buoyancy, and joyousness that seemed perennial. How we shall miss her exquisite sense of humor that frequently dispelled our perplexities! Often, after spending a night of sleeplessness attended with pain, she would come into the family the next morning as fresh as a dewdrop and relate some bright incident, or in some other way put the entire household in a delightful humor. Upon surprise being expressed at her cheerfulness, she would say: "I never could mope; I am so glad the morning has come." She instinctively recognized the best there was in every member of a family, and honored it, thus becoming a perpetual benediction in one's home. Little children bloomed about her like flowers and wreathed about her like vines, while the aged found her ever their thoughtful and considerate friend. In society she was a pleasing conversationalist, and showed herself well versed on the topics of the day.

We remember seeing her upon one occasion at a social gathering. She was dressed with her accustomed exquisite taste in black satin with trimmings of dainty white lace and a bunch of violets. Her grace of person and her witty, vivacious conversation made her universally admired. Strangers remarked: "Who is that sweet woman? She is quite irresistible." Her delicate taste and refinement forbade her making any reference to her religious work when there was no occasion for it. She did not oppress strangers with details of her mission and try to convince them of theirs. In short, she was not a "hobbyist."

Humility was a very marked and ever-present characteristic of her nature. So far from being elated and filled with a spirit of self-righteousness because of her marvelous success, she seemed to grow humbler as her pathway widened toward the infinite shore, and to sink out of her own sight as she got a larger vision of the meanings of life. She did not talk much about religion unless the way was opened for it, but she lived it and breathed it and knew no life outside of Christ. Without making any effort to do so, she frequently put truths into a concise form that crystallized in one's mind to stay. For example, her criticism of those who taught promiscuously "faith healing" was given

in one sentence, and contained more than whole
sermons of denunciations: " They have too much
faith in the faith instead of in God." A prominent trait of Miss Helm's character that com-
manded universal esteem was her independence of
thought. Dr. Alexander says, in speaking of her:
" She was what few people are or ever become:
a thinker, original and independent. She accepted nothing because somebody else thought it
or said it. It must become clear to her own mind.
She considered and canvassed and settled for
herself every item of her theological belief, and
accordingly had a form of statement for each doc-
trine she accepted that was peculiarly her own.
This does not mean that she was unreceptive or
not open to conviction. Whatever was made clear
to her thought as a correction of her views she
welcomed as such. But I have met few people in
my life who, in the investigation of new views or
doctrines, could ask more searching questions or
apply more rigorous tests, and I have in more than
one instance had to abandon or modify views that
were brought under the test of her penetrating
thought. I should say in estimating her character
that she was predominantly intellectual, although I
say it with a good deal of hesitancy, for there are
not many who have the intensity of nature and the
depth of feeling which she had, and fewer still
who are as spiritual as she was. The simplicity,
purity, and beauty of her faith were almost ideal.

She said at one time that she had never been without the consciousness of the Fatherhood of God since her early childhood, and added: 'Those two words, "my Father," are to me the sweetest words in human language.'"

The last distinctive feature of Miss Helm's remarkable personality to which we call attention was her profound appreciation of the love of her friends. One would not expect that a woman with such a career as hers would have been melted to tears by the gift of a flower. Yet this was repeatedly the case. Love never grew old to her, nor ever came as a matter of course. It was as fresh and refreshing as the morning dews, and she always received it with gratitude. Her nature made it a necessity for her to love, and love went out from her great heart naturally and broadly like a full-flowing river; but when she realized the response in other hearts, it gave her a sense of sweet surprise and delight. How her friends valued her letters! Some of them were poems in prose, and all were pervaded with love as genuine and full for each as if bestowed on no other. The following extracts are but a few of the many that could be given to illustrate.

Upon one occasion, two summers ago, she wrote from her old home at Elizabethtown: "Dear, dear friend, it is a lovely Sabbath evening, and as I sit here enjoying it all it seems so appropriate that I should be writing to you.

Everything around me is so beautiful, and the birds are singing softly, one at a time, as if not to break the quiet of the evening. It reminds me of Mrs. Southey's little poem on "Sunday Evening," beginning

There's a sacred, soothing sweetness
In a Sabbath eve like this.

The old place here is looking particularly beautiful this summer. It is kept in such exquisite order, and the flower-beds are so bright with their wealth of flowers. It is all very restful, and I only want to look and breathe. Your sweet letter was a cordial to my heart. I am so thankful that there are some hearts into which I can creep down and be at home. Is there anything like the goodness of God? I should like to spend a summer that suited both of us with you, and perhaps this may come to pass sometime, somewhere. In the mean time we will rest in each other's love and wait for our Father's direction."

After her return from the seashore that summer, she writes: "I have thoroughly enjoyed my summer trips and visits, even if I have not gained in strength, and that is something in this life of ours. Everybody has been so sweet and loving to me. Truly God is good to me to give me so many kind friends. I do not deserve this, yet I am so glad of it. I was with such kind people in Wilmington, who did a great deal for my pleasure, and my stay in Beaufort, on the Sound, was like a dream. The sails on the beautiful water were so quiet, so soft, gliding on between the water and the blue sky; the yellow-green islands lying here and there like bits of fairy-land, smiling back memories of far-away childhood fancies, when only the murmur of the conch-shell was all I knew of the sea. I have brought some shells for little Ruth, and shall tell her of the sea as it was once told to me. I wonder if it will awaken the longing to see it as with me. I have much to talk about and to tell you when I see you."

She wrote from Florida, in March, 1897: " I have accepted an invitation from Mrs. Hargrove to visit her during the time from my return to our going to the annual meeting. We want to consult each other about many things."

She returned from Florida very weak and frail. Although she had in the spring expected to make other plans, she remained in Bishop Hargrove's home, a more than welcome member of the household, during the entire summer and into the autumn, when she was called to her home above.

Late in the summer she writes that she had been very ill, and had thought it was her last illness— the end seemed so near—yet her Father had led her out again, and she knew by that that her work was not quite done. She then adds: " Sometimes our Father draws us aside to rest a while with him. I am so glad you are having a rest in a sweet, quiet place. There must be a time for the still small voice to speak when our hearts can hear. The bustle of going, going, with the crowds and hearing only the din and noise about us not only wearies the heart, but it gradually weakens our powers of hearing the higher tones and deadens the susceptibility of our souls to impressions direct from God."

As the summer waned she grew weaker, although she continued her work and frequently attended the Centennial Exposition at Nashville. But she seemed to be conscious, during the entire time, that the end was near, and to one friend she wrote, when on the very threshold of her Father's house, November 5: "I can not tell you how sweet your letter was to me. I thank God for prompting you to write it. To know that my spiritual sisters so love me is indeed a great reward for the feeble efforts I have made to serve our common Lord and Saviour. If it is an earnest of the heavenly love, how full of joy our Father's home will be! I do not know, dear friend, whether my stay here will be long or short. It may be that my Master will see that it is necessary for his glory for me to drag along wearily as now, using me, perhaps in ways I know not of, to help others in their journey homeward. If so, his will is mine. I know that he will comfort and help me always; but should he deem it wisest to take me home very soon, I shall be glad. My heart, homesick, trembles with a strange joy at the bare

thought of it. I wait his commands, hoping to
hear the call: 'Come home.' In the mean time
knowing that I am going some day helps me to be
brave and cheerful as the days go by. His child
should not mope and fear because he asks her to
wait a while and to do him a bit of service that
perhaps another can not do. I have but weakness, yet he uses it. I am sick, yet he sees that
some one looks after my comfort, and so he uses
that too. My poor woman's heart longs for love;
he lavishes it upon me through the Comforter and
through my dear sisters in his love. My heart is
resting and waiting for him.''

The last text marked in her Bible was on November 12: "I must work the works of him that
sent me, while it is day: the night cometh, when
no man can work." And she did work, even at
her office, on that day and on Saturday. During
the Sabbath she remained in her room. What
transpired in the sanctuary of her soul during that
last Sabbath it is not for us to know, but we may
be assured that her hand was laid in the hand of
her Father while her spirit held sweet communion
with him.

On Monday the kind solicitations of her friends,
Bishop and Mrs. Hargrove, were much appreciated by her, but she expressed a desire to remain alone. And this she did during the entire
day. Alone with the past as it came to her,
flooding her with memories of far-off, beautiful

childhood, of the girlhood possessed by a noble ambition, of the ripened womanhood filled with long years of toil and service in the Master's vineyard—such willing toil, such happy service! Alone with the future that could hold nothing but a fuller revelation of her Father's love; that even then glowed with the light of heaven as she watched with tremulous joy for the messenger who she knew would soon come for her. As the shadows gathered deep that night, in the hush of the valley of silence, an angel met her, bearing the tokens of a "golden bowl broken and a silver cord loosed," and she followed him without grief or fear.

No tender yet sad farewell
  For her quiv'ring lips was heard.
So softly she crossed the stream,
  'Twas scarce by a ripple stirred.

She was spared all pain of tears,
  She was spared all mortal strife;
It was not death—she passed
  In a moment to endless life.

Weep not for the swift release
  From earthly pain and care,
Nor grieve that she reached her home
  E'er she knew that she was there.

But think of her sweet surprise,
  The sudden and strange delight,
As she met her Saviour's smile
  And walked with him in white.

12

IN MEMORIAM.

A SONG OF FAITH.

EMILY M. ALLEN.

January 1, 1898.

"Behold, I make all things new." (Rev. xxi. 5.)

The New-Year joy is on the earth again,
Again we face the glorious, sun-flushed east
Where gray Eternity becomes our roseate Time,
That we may have companionship with it—
We lowly children of the Infinite One—
And come to know at last, through days and years,
The vast inheritance that is our own.
O joy of human life! O blessedness to be!
Oh, sweet the things forever old yet new?
That God is God is truth enough for earth.
To this I hold, 'neath winter skies of gray,
Mid wild north winds and leafless, shuddering trees
Which usher in the year that is to be;
And holding this, old things are all made new.

And thou, beloved, with us here no more,
On whom our changing years can have no power,
Who knowest no time but Love's eternal Now,
Couldst thou but speak from out the shining ones
That haste in faith to do His loving will,
Wouldst not thou say, "O friends, 'tis true!
That God is God is truth enough for heaven.
Be strong down there to work His loving will
Among His sorrowful, poor, and sinful ones.
If hearts grow faint at wrongs long unredressed,
At old, old ills that keep the world in night,
Oh, lift your faces to the light that falls!
Remember God is God, and hear him say,
'Because I am I shall make all things new.'"

—*Memorial Number Our Homes.*